'Told with heartbreaking clarity, [these] stories are hard to forget.' *Choice*

'A dark, tragic story with the resilient light of humanity shining through it... It truly spoke to my soul.'   *Marjorie's World of Books*

'Grjasnowa provides a close-as-skin understanding of what it's like to suffer bombardment, torture, and dislocation while remaining human and hopeful... Highly recommended.'
Library Journal

'Grjasnowa's measured, undemonstrative writing style (the book is beautifully translated from German by Katy Derbyshire) is central to the novel's success... A significant literary and moral success.'   *Big Issue*

'A superb writer and storyteller, Olga Grjasnowa...takes her readers on a heartbreaking journey along the streets of war-torn Damascus and on to Europe.'   *European Literature Network*

'Olga Grjasnowa writes from the nerve center of her generation.'
Die Zeit

'An important and painful book.'   *Deutschlandradio Kultur*

'There are few authors writing in German as sensuously and vividly as Grjasnowa.'   *Spiegel Kultur*

'Olga Grjasnowa's sentences crack like a whip.'
Süddeutsche Zeitung

'It is wonderful that there are writers like Grjasnowa who can write brilliantly and decisively about the real world.'   *Brigitte*

CITY

of

JASMINE

Olga Grjasnowa

*Translated from the German
by Katy Derbyshire*

ONEWORLD

A Oneworld Book

First published in North America, Great Britain and Australia by
Oneworld Publications, 2019

This mass market paperback edition published 2020

Originally published in German as *Gott ist nicht schüchtern* by Aufbau Verlag, 2017

Co-funded by the
Creative Europe Programme
of the European Union

The European Commission support for the production of this publication
does not constitute an endorsement of the contents which reflects the views
only of the authors, and the Commission cannot be held responsible for
any use which may be made of the information contained therein.

The translation of this work was supported by a grant from the Goethe-Institut.

Paperback ISBN 978-1-78607-703-5
eBook ISBN 978-1-78607-488-1

Typeset by Fakenham Prepress Solutions, Fakenham, Norfolk NR21 8NL
Printed and bound in Great Britain by Clays Ltd, Elcograf S.p.A.

Oneworld Publications
10 Bloomsbury Street
London WC1B 3SR
England

Stay up to date with the latest books,
special offers, and exclusive content from
Oneworld with our newsletter

Sign up on our website
oneworld-publications.com

For Ayham

PART I

The first fields are already visible through the plane window, followed by an ocean of houses that vanishes again; then the wing slews upwards and the window reveals nothing but sky blue. The plane rights itself and Hammoudi sees a field scorched by the sun. The wheels hit the ground with a jolt.

Damascus's international airport has barely changed since Hammoudi's last visit. The border guards in the dilapidated cabins are as bad tempered as ever. They scrutinize his passport dourly and point out that it expires in a few days' time.

'That's why I'm here,' says Hammoudi. A guard in a poorly fitting uniform shoos him away.

Hammoudi likes being in Syria, with certain reservations. All his life he's been told there's no future here and he ought to emigrate to Canada, Australia or Europe after his degree, if not sooner. The life he'd lived in Syria had confirmed those reservations.

The luggage takes a long time to arrive. Several large families lose patience; children start whining; a gentleman with salt-and-pepper hair lights a cigarette and gets ticked off by security guards; cleaning women walk to and fro with their water pails, deliberately slow and not cleaning anything. When the light above the baggage carousel finally goes on, everyone crowds around the beginning of the conveyor belt and tries to secure a strategic position; two blond men with reddish beards speaking loud Swiss German win in the end. As the belt starts moving at last, a murmur goes up in the crowd. The luggage is quickly retrieved. Bags, suitcases, bundles, backpacks and boxes are heaved off, placed on luggage trolleys and pushed towards the exit with a sense of euphoria.

A crowd of people wait behind the barrier in Arrivals, looking out for friends and relatives and storming towards them as soon as the door to baggage reclaim opens even a crack. A police officer repeatedly warns them not to get too close to the door. Faces alternate in rapid succession between joy, curiosity and dismay. Children stand around clutching balloons, babies rub their tired eyes as fathers wave bouquets of flowers.

Hammoudi is welcomed by his own rowdy group, although he had actually intended to take a taxi straight to his hotel. He'd like a little peace and quiet – two nights of sleeping alone, far away from Claire and from his family waiting for him in Deir ez-Zor. A brief time out, just for himself. That's why he didn't tell his friends in Damascus his arrival time. They interpreted his silence as forgetfulness and simply looked up the landing time online. Now they wrap him in hugs and kiss him on the cheeks. Hammoudi is loaded into a car, complete with his heavy case full of gifts.

Although it's outside his budget, Hammoudi has booked a room at the Four Seasons. It was only weeks ago that he completed his residency as a reconstructive surgeon in Paris with honours. He'd spent five years working towards that moment and when it finally came it felt as though he was entitled to it. Then he applied to the city's three best hospitals and was soon invited to interviews at each one. Hammoudi was tall, slim, courteous and charming. His French was flawless. The decisive factor, though, was his perfect facial symmetry – he was just the man people trusted to have internalized established beauty norms. He quickly decided on the hospital that made him the best offer and immediately received a contract in the post. That evening, he'd celebrated by treating his girlfriend Claire to an expensive dinner with plenty of champagne.

After that he booked a trip to Syria to renew his passport – a mere formality, but his residency permit in France depended on it, so he thought he'd take the opportunity for a short holiday.

The marble floors of the Four Seasons lobby glint with cleanliness and the copious flower arrangements exude a morbid scent. Two security men check Hammoudi's papers, almost refusing to let him into the hotel because he's not a foreigner. His friends are coming to pick him up again in two hours; he asked them to give him time for a nap and a shower.

His room is luxurious, the bed wide and firm, the sheets bright white and freshly pressed, the minibar well stocked and the furnishings in Damascene style. A voluminous bouquet on the side table at least smells better than the arrangements downstairs. Hammoudi runs a bath and dials Claire's number.

That evening he goes out with his friends. A noisy group in their mid-thirties, women and men; some married, others already divorced or simply single, lesbians or in the kind of relationships that don't entail commitments. They tour the centre of Damascus, heading into bars, drinking arak, ordering small dishes, more arak and more food. They laugh, scream, bitch and argue. They're louder than they used to be, trying to reforge the ties between them, to assure each other they haven't been forgotten, they're still good friends.

Hammoudi makes an effort to catch up on his friends' lives, to remember each of their partners, children and career updates, but his head is soon buzzing. He doesn't know that his old uni clique is only meeting up now because of him – they've drifted apart in the years of his absence.

At first they're all awkward, their interactions clumsy, but after a while they relax, not least due to the alcohol. They recall

events from their younger days, juggling names of acquaintances, streets and places that Hammoudi barely remembers.

Damascus, too, is hardly recognizable to him. The city centre
has been gentrified over the past five years – tiny grocery shops
forced to close and the spaces reopened as Zara or Benetton;
bakeries making way for cafés serving soy-milk cappuccinos at
European prices; shops that once sold absolutely everything,
from screwdrivers to petrol canisters, replaced by mobile
phone stores.

As the next day breaks, Hammoudi collapses into his overpriced hotel bed and instantly falls asleep. Through the window,
the curses of drunken night owls mingle with the muezzin's
call to morning prayers.

Amal tries to act the fear away. She's spent her whole life studying the people around her: family, friends, lovers, complete strangers. She has memorized their facial expressions and gestures so as to reproduce them precisely on stage. She has learned characters, vocal pitches and emotions. Even as a tiny child not yet capable of speech, she imitated people. And yet it took her a long time to admit she wanted to be an actor. She thought she wasn't talented or pretty enough for the stage. She thought her hips were too wide, her nose too long and her voice not firm enough. Aside from that, her father always implied acting was not a profession for honourable women. Amal got a degree in English literature but books weren't enough for her, so one day she auditioned for the prestigious Institute of Dramatic Arts.

All that seems long ago now. Fear has settled in like a parasite building a nest inside her ribs. Amal knows exactly what might happen to her but she doesn't know when or whether it will come about, and it's this uncertainty that makes her tremble. Too many people around her have been arrested or tortured or have simply disappeared, which amounts to the same thing.

Damascus is a noisy city, messy and hectic, overflowing with buses and taxis hooting, the yells of street vendors, the humming of the air conditioners on the outsides of houses, all mixed with the loud music streaming out of bars and car windows. In Damascus, a person can drown in history and its superlatives. Today, though, the city is submerged in uncanny silence. No traffic, no conversations, not even a whisper to be heard. The sky is decked in grey clouds.

Amal keeps looking over at the secret-service men, her body registering their every movement and sound. The curtain in a window of the house opposite twitches. An old woman is trying to peer around the heavy damask drapes as inconspicuously as possible, and at that moment Amal decides she never wants to hide behind a curtain again, not today, not tomorrow and not in forty years' time; and the only way to achieve that is to stay put in this square, come what may.

The first demonstration took place two days ago. It was the first time since winter that the air had felt mild, almost warm. Amal and a few of her friends headed for the parliament building with A4 cardboard signs. Amal's scarf was pulled down low over her face. They hadn't dared to take the placards out of their bags. At the end of the demonstration they avoided eye contact and dispersed as quickly as they could. They were ashamed to be running away in secrecy after a demonstration while people in other countries were setting themselves alight.

During the early days of the revolution, the optimists thought the global media and Al Jazeera would report on their demonstrations. They didn't think the international community would abandon them when they were only demanding of their state what it seemed the rest of the world wanted of it, too. No one was really thinking of toppling the regime – they merely wanted reforms. A few minor concessions.

People were sick and tired. Amal was tired, her brother was tired, her friends, her fellow students, acquaintances, strangers in the streets, the entire vulgar *bohème* was sick and tired. They were sick and tired of the corruption, the secret services' arbitrary decisions, their own powerlessness and permanent humiliation. They were sick and tired of all public libraries, airports, stadiums, universities, parks and even kindergartens being named after the Assads. They were sick and tired of their fathers, brothers and uncles mouldering in jails. They were sick and tired of the whole family having to chip in to buy the sons out of military service while the North American teenagers on cable TV were given cars by their parents and travelled the world. They were sick and tired of reciting 'Assad for all eternity' every morning at school and swearing to fight all Americans, Zionists and imperialists. They were sick and tired of memorizing Assad quotes in political-education classes and then filling in the gaps in the right order for their tests. They were sick and tired of being taught in military education to dismantle and reassemble a machine gun. They were sick and tired of being treated like animals. And above all they were sick and tired of not being allowed to say any of it out loud.

Amal's generation is the first to know nothing other than the Assad clan's totalitarian rule. Unlike their parents and grand-parents, who well remember the endless putsches before Hafez al-Assad seized power, or the 1982 massacre of the Muslim Brothers in Hama, a clear signal from the government that it was not to be trifled with. Since then, the Assad regime has behaved like an establishment ordained by God. More than that, Bashar al-Assad is greater than God, or at least that's what's implied by his omnipresence and that of his father, brother, wife and three children – with portraits in even the furthest corner of the country, like scarecrows to frighten and dispel his subjects.

The next demonstration. Out of the corner of her eye, Amal spots the Alawi actor Fadwa Soliman, a woman she's long admired, and for a moment the sight reassures her. She takes a deep breath and wraps one hand around the other to stop the trembling. No one knows what will happen next. The regime might make an example of the demonstrators this time, arresting them all or using violence to break up the crowd.

After a long time, during which the demonstrators do nothing but stand together and watch the secret-service men, a small man in an oversized leather jacket leaves the group and heads for the nearest café. He's one of the most high-profile artists in Syria. Amal and around twenty others tail after him like a throng of children, relieved to have evaded danger.

Al Rawda, meaning Garden of Eden, is a traditional Damascus café serving alcohol and small dishes, frequented primarily by opposition activists, gays, lesbians, young lovers and petty criminals. The demonstrators gather in the garden, which sometimes does seem like a paradise, with its impressive marble arches and palm trees. They talk openly, albeit in extremely hypothetical form, about concessions by the regime, and they flirt more blatantly than ever. Having greeted everyone she knows, Amal goes to the toilet, runs cold water over her wrists, splashes her face and breathes deeply in and out. Her body shakes as the tension leaves her. She's astounded that the demonstration went so calmly. Amal has never felt as though she belongs to a particular group but for the first time the thought of doing so doesn't unsettle her.

Hammoudi's family celebrates his arrival in Deir ez-Zor with a huge party. The courtyard is full of uncles, aunts, cousins, nephews and nieces. He had forgotten how stressful a large family can be. The girls are wearing hairbands and frou-frou dresses, squealing as the boys chase them. Then they switch over, the boys running away and the girls pursuing them with even more squeals.

A giant table is set up in the middle of the courtyard, straining under the weight of all the food and drink. Hammoudi's father has had a lamb slaughtered, stuffed with rice and nuts and then slowly roasted over the fire in the yard. His mother instructed the staff to spend several days preparing salads and starters, marinating seven kilos of kebab meat and various fish, stirring yoghurt and setting out huge trays of baklava and *shaabiyat* pastries.

Their game momentarily interrupted, a crowd of children mobs Hammoudi as he hands out the gifts he brought from France. His aunts load generous portions for all the guests onto delicate porcelain plates that Hammoudi's mother imported from Japan. His grandparents have seven daughters and not a single son, something his aunts and his grandfather in particular consider a great blessing. He sent all his daughters to university and all seven of them chose medicine. Now they work in different fields but are still inseparable. Throughout his childhood summers, Hammoudi saw his aunts huddled together on the roof of their house, eating nuts and sweets as they gossiped about the neighbours.

Hammoudi's cousin pours two fingers of clear liquid into each of their glasses, adds ice cubes and dilutes the alcohol with water, turning the drink milky white. The neighbours are there too, a couple whose son Mohammed, once a chubby boy, has grown into a lanky teenager who dreams of building bridges.

Hammoudi watches his brother talking excitedly to a girl and smiles to himself – Naji is always on the lookout for a wife, even though he's not exactly the youngest at thirty-three. He's the black sheep of the family.

After the meal, Hammoudi's grandmother reads the coffee grounds. A long queue forms before the fragile woman bent low from arthritis, who patiently inspects one cup after another and interprets the brown remains. She is one of the few fortune tellers who don't predict bridegrooms and sons for young girls. She sees a fish, meaning money, in one of Hammoudi's female cousins' coffee cups. Hammoudi takes his cup over too; his grandmother strokes his brow but then her eyes darken and she stares at his cup for so long that Hammoudi asks her with a laugh whether his future is really that black.

'God will decide,' she says in the end. '*Min timmi ila abau' al-samah.*' From my mouth to the gates of paradise.

Later that evening, Hammoudi asks her again about his future, but his grandmother merely shakes her head and asks for a glass of water.

The morning after the party, while the rest of the household is still asleep, Hammoudi sets out for the municipal administration to get his passport renewed. The security men wave him through, drowsy at this early hour. The corridors are narrow, the walls painted pale yellow and decorated with a bright green border. Hammoudi takes a seat in a stuffy room and waits for his name to be called.

The waiting rooms of the Syrian Republic have much in common with its prisons – no one knows how long they'll spend inside them. Time here comes in uncertain dimensions, it stretches out or trickles away. Perhaps a whole day will pass, perhaps only half an hour. Hammoudi tries out all kinds of ways to pass the time, games on his phone, emails, a novel he started months ago; and yet his body is in a permanent state of alert, waiting for his name to be called at any moment.

Three hours later, he's permitted to enter a tiny room and hand his passport over to a civil servant in a not-quite-fresh white shirt. The wooden desk is piled high with files, some of them already coated in a layer of dust. Above the desk hangs a large portrait of President Bashar al-Assad, its colours already faded. The man nods and says, 'Come back at four. Then you can collect your passport.'

The outside light dazzles Hammoudi and he swiftly dons his sunglasses, which look too elegant and expensive for Deir ez-Zor. His entire wardrobe is unsuited for this city, he thinks. His mother even put out a freshly ironed jellabiya for him last night. He makes use of the time for a walk around town, which now seems otherworldly to him, as does his whole childhood. The streets are empty at this hour; many of the residents are taking a midday nap and dogs too are dozing in the shade, while cats rummage untiringly through the rubbish containers.

Hammoudi buys a lighter and cigarettes in a tiny super-market. The shopkeeper is in a drunken stupor behind the counter when he comes in, the security-camera monitor and an old TV showing a football match flickering beside his shaven head. Hammoudi glances at the game and tries to make out the teams. Then he tears the cellophane from the pack and hungrily inserts a cigarette between his lips.

He pulls his jacket tighter around his body and continues his walk. It's still cool but the temperature rises to over forty degrees in the shade during the summer. Deir ez-Zor is known as the 'yellow city' as sand covers the streets and houses for two hundred and twenty days of the year. Even the sky takes on a saffron hue, shifting to a stark shade of red as the evening approaches.

Hammoudi can't resist any more, he is drawn to the Euphrates, the emerald-green river revered by the locals like a deity. He strolls at an easy pace and stops at the banks, keeping the suspension bridge in view. He watches a handful of boys, obviously playing truant, leaping into the water. Their dives are dangerous because the current is strong, but it's an old ritual among the city's youth. Everyone knows at least one family who has lost a relative to the river, but that doesn't stop the boys.

Hammoudi thinks he recognizes Mohammed among the divers, and is reminded that it's not actually a suspension bridge but a cable-stayed bridge; Mohammed explained it to him once. The boy who might be Mohammed raises his arms above his head and lets himself fall. Hammoudi waits for his head to reappear on the water's surface and then turns around.

He's back in the waiting room by ten to four. This time he's called straight into the department head's office, where the man gives him a stern look and announces, 'You can have your passport back but you're not allowed to leave the country.'

'Pardon?' Hammoudi responds.

'The Security Service has some concerns about letting you leave the country again. Please contact the relevant authority.'

'But the Syrian embassy assured me I could just get my passport renewed. It wasn't a big deal, they told me.'

'Where was that?'

'In Paris.'

'Then go and see my colleagues in Paris.'

'But I'd have to leave the country first!'

'I'm not going to get into a discussion.' His face devoid of expression, the civil servant flips open the next file.

Amal is walking through the Al-Hamidiyah Souq with her childhood friend Luna. Dusk is falling, though the sky is still bright. The first mosquitoes are gathering in the cones of light beneath the streetlamps. The air smells of jasmine, incense, rose oil, handmade soap and heaps of spices: liquorice, dried coriander, tarragon, paprika, turmeric, cinnamon and *za'atar*, rose petals, lavender, borage. The market is made up of countless small lanes and corridors leading to different sections, including several aisles where only clothes or household items are sold. Everything is piled high with wares, often spread out on carpets and plastic sheets in front of the shops.

Amal's and Luna's mothers once brought them here in their prams, strolling side by side. Now the two of them are looking for lingerie that might appeal to Luna's new lover. Several lanes in the Al-Hamidiyah Souq sell underwear for prospective brides. With their customers consisting mainly of curious Syrian women, Western tourists and mature ladies from the Arab Emirates, the shops put up a virtuous front while in fact they resemble Dutch sex shops. The sales staff are all men in their late sixties.

Amal and Luna stop outside various shop windows, looking at whips and bras; some S&M-like creations, some with flashing lights and some with holes at nipple level. They giggle and exchange whispers like little girls, even though they're both in their mid-twenties and each lost their virginity aged fifteen and fourteen. When a slight drizzle sets in they finally go inside one of the shops.

A man with a large nose offers them a coffee and asks whether one of them is the bride. Luna nods a bit too eagerly. A teenage boy with braces on his teeth brings a tray of coffee cups and a sugar bowl from the back room.

'You have the figure of a young girl, it won't be hard to find the right thing for you, sister,' the salesman says, blatantly eyeing up Luna. She still looks like a fourteen-year-old – she's thin with long hair that falls over her face. All her outfits are either slightly too tight or too loose, making her look by turns like a Lolita trying on her mother's dresses or a child grown out of her clothes.

Five minutes later, he has spread his entire range out for them. The table is spilling over with chocolate thongs, sequinned, string tangas, and tiny lacy items decorated with feathers or whole insects. There are thongs featuring pictures of superheroes and electronic extras; some play a love song, others just 'Old MacDonald Had a Farm'. The salesman clearly enjoys smugly explaining even the slightest detail. But Luna is a difficult customer, indecisive and tight-fisted.

'Sister, as I said, you can wear anything with your figure,' the salesman says, 'but I'd still recommend a push-up; sometimes men just want that little bit more.'

'No.' Luna doesn't elaborate, but she sips thoughtfully at her coffee and frowns.

'Look, sister, these are new in.' The man drapes a series of bra-and-panties sets in front of Luna. The bottom halves are patterned with brightly coloured birds.

'*Ish al-asfour*,' Amal whispers and the man grins – the Arabic term for 'bird's nest' also refers to a woman's pubic hair.

'Some like it fuller, especially in Europe, so I'm told,' the man explains and then suddenly holds up a thong with a rose on it, the Hezbollah symbol. 'This one, perhaps?' he asks hopefully.

Luna pulls a face and flaps her hands, angry now. The almost non-existent piece of clothing vanishes back beneath the counter in haste.

'How about this, sister? When you present yourself to your husband in this, don't take the bra off yourself, wait until he goes to undo it and then clap your hands, and the bra unfastens automatically and the panties slip down on their own.'

The sales talk is fortunately interrupted when a woman wearing a floor-length abaya comes in and enquires in English after the latest push-up bras. Her husband and teenage son wait outside.

Another woman buys a pair of knickers with a huge chocolate heart attached, and Amal whispers, 'Pretty clear instructions, for once.'

In the end, Luna does purchase several ensembles for her latest affair. More amused than concerned, Amal asks, 'Do you think it's all really necessary?'

'The man's been married for seven years, of course it's necessary,' Luna hisses.

Over the next few weeks, Hammoudi's family tries everything to get him permission to leave the country. They contact all the generals, functionaries and secret-service men they know and have been showering with precautionary gifts for years, but no one can say why his exit permit has been revoked. For the time being, he has to stay in Syria. He loses his job in the seventh arrondissement before he can even start work.

He calls Claire regularly. Her voice sounds tired and saccharine and Hammoudi recalls her naked body, longing for her firm thighs, small breasts and magical hands. She got the best results in their university year. Hammoudi always came second.

He hasn't told her he can't return to France. Up to now, she's believed there are merely 'difficulties with his passport' and has drawn her own conclusions. He knows she won't come and join him. She'd never move to a country at war with Israel. Hammoudi senses he'll soon have to let her go. But at the moment he's still trying to postpone that decision. Just one more day, he tells himself every morning, full of naïve hope.

They first met at the Pierre and Marie Curie University. Claire stood out from the crowd, being taller than most of the men in their year, with long, black hair and large dark-blue eyes. Hammoudi was convinced she was an Arab but when he spoke to her in Arabic in the cafeteria she merely stared at him in surprise, shook her head and walked away.

Some time later, they met again at a dinner party. He smiled at her first, then they talked, and in the end they danced. But still, for months Claire wouldn't consider going out with him; she was engaged to an older Jewish consultant who kept kosher and prayed in the synagogue on holy days. When Hammoudi professed his love to Claire she responded merely that there was nothing she could do about it.

But Hammoudi would not be put off and kept asking Claire out, to the cinema, to a restaurant, a concert, the theatre or an exhibition. Then he suggested daytime trips, to the planetarium, the zoo, a swimming pool, and at some point 'no' gradually gave way to a 'yes'. It didn't take long for Claire to leave the consultant and move into Hammoudi's miniscule flat near the Gare du Nord. Every morning, Hammoudi reached out for her before fully waking. He still couldn't quite believe she'd chosen him.

They were together for five years and those were the happiest years of his life. Claire challenged him in every respect, never satisfied and always wanting Hammoudi to make more of an effort, in their relationship and in his work. Hammoudi liked that, and Claire liked his devotion, as she'd tell her girlfriends – only half-joking. When they both came home from the hospital in the evenings they'd go out to eat together and discuss their cases. Claire questioned his diagnoses and scrutinized his treatment methods, and for the first time in his life Hammoudi had an external perspective of himself and a partner on an equal footing, someone who took him seriously and criticized him.

After their first year together, Claire began gradually integrating Hammoudi into her family. She introduced him to her parents and her four older brothers, all of whom were married with several children. Hammoudi accompanied Claire to the kosher Seder evenings at her parents' house and to her nieces' and nephews' countless birthdays. He felt comfortable around Claire's relatives. They were a total contrast to his own family – quiet and reserved, distant yet warm – but they gave Hammoudi a chance to recover from his noisy aunts, who meddled in everything and were constantly asking when he was going to get married.

Five months ago, Hammoudi finally decided to propose to Claire. He didn't really want to get married but he assumed that was exactly what Claire and her family expected of him. He carried the diamond ring around with him for weeks before he finally found the right opportunity. He popped the question in the garden of the Rodin Museum and Claire answered without hesitating. She loved him, she said, but she didn't want to get married. Hammoudi felt foolish and rejected but he went on exactly as before and never mentioned his failed proposal to anyone. Even now, Hammoudi can't imagine a life without Claire, let alone one in Syria. He spends his days in the family home or in the city's many bars, never letting his phone out of his sight. He hasn't given up hope, but nothing changes.

Hammoudi liked the Parisian charm. He liked the people there, friendly but never intrusive. He couldn't resist the city's beauty, the architecture, the tiny overpriced bistros and cafés, the locals' smug self-satisfaction. On their days off, Hammoudi and Claire would roam the museums. She would point out a picture, explain to Hammoudi what she saw and then put the painting in its historical context, a habit learned from her art-dealer parents. Then she'd add a quiet postscript about when she'd first seen the work and what it meant to her. Hammoudi thought he loved her more after every museum visit.

One night, Hammoudi has a dream. Claire comes home and can't find him but he hears her calling for him, her voice first far away and then coming closer, fading, coming closer again. When she finally enters the kitchen, Hammoudi screams and kicks. Only now does he realize he has shrunk and been shut inside the fridge. He treads water while his strength ebbs away.

Then Claire finally opens the fridge door, the electric light goes on and Hammoudi tries to grab onto a piece of carrot with the last of his energy – for some reason he's swimming in a pan of soup. He calls out for help, getting cramp in his leg. But when Claire finally sees him and tries to fish him out she ends up suddenly swimming in the liquid alongside him. Drenched in sweat, he wakes at dawn. His lips taste of stock.

Amal only has a very few memories of her mother but strangely enough, one of them is of her mother cooking. The kitchen was a wasted room for Svetlana; if she did deign to enter it, she'd usually make a Russian concoction with the oddly French-sounding name of Olivier salad, a mixture of overcooked vegetables and sausage. The salad's special ingredients were tinned peas, which were hard to get hold of in both Moscow and Damascus, and tons of greasy mayonnaise, which drowned out any remaining flavour. While she cooked, Svetlana talked on the phone to one of her many girlfriends, the telephone cable wrapped loosely around one hand, a cigarette in the other. It was not uncommon for ash to land in the food.

Back then, Amal's family lived in a parallel Russian world. They had Russian friends – mostly men with thick moustaches and thicker waistlines who worked as professors at Syrian universities. They spent their holidays at their grandparents' summer house near St Petersburg, and on New Year's Eve they had a tree, a bottle of sparkling wine and a bag of mandarins. Their parents spoke Russian to each other, as Bassel had studied in the Soviet Union for five years on a grant and learned the language perfectly. Svetlana spoke Arabic with such a strong Russian accent that strangers could barely understand her.

As a child, Amal idolized her mother, a strikingly beautiful woman who was loving and caring, though not necessarily reliable. In the few faded photos that Amal has left of her, Svetlana looks elegant and very feminine. She is blonde with blue eyes, wears strappy sandals or court shoes; her dresses are cut in classic styles and her skirts always emphasize her svelte legs. Amal's favourite picture shows Svetlana on a trip to Saudi Arabia, wearing an unusual abaya decorated with fine French lace and wafting gently about her body in the wind, her hair covered casually with a black scarf and large sunglasses lending her the required sophistication.

Svetlana, meaning 'light' in Russian, fell in love with a young Syrian, at the box office of the Leningrad Philharmonic Hall. They spent seven hours waiting side by side for cheap tickets for seats in the gods, branded as rats and vultures by the mousy Soviet theatre supervisors and not even going to the toilet in case they lost their places in the queue. When the last remaining tickets were finally sold Svetlana was left empty-handed, but Bassel heroically sacrificed his seat to her. After the performance he was waiting for her in the foyer and suggested walking her home. It wasn't safe on the streets, he said, and he was right.

Bassel studied engineering in the Soviet Union, and Svetlana fell pregnant shortly before his final exams. They married and Svetlana gave birth to Amal in Damascus, then her brother Ali a few years later. But when Amal was eleven her parents divorced and Svetlana went back to Russia without the children – Syrian law automatically gave the father custody.

Amal and Ali had not had a chance to say goodbye to their mother. Bassel had sent them to distant relatives in Saudi Arabia one summer and by the time they returned, sunburnt and religiously schooled, Svetlana had vanished without a trace. Her belongings were gone, as were most of her photos. Amal only managed to save a few of them, which she happened to find in a drawer a year after Svetlana's disappearance. Bassel must have overlooked them.

He had explained at the time that their mother had died. No one told them what she died of, all their questions were ignored. There was no grave, no grieving friends or other indications of a death, but Amal never questioned her father and she believed what he said. For years, she wept for her mother. Until one moonless night, shortly before Amal was to lose her virginity, Bassel told her Svetlana had left the family and was now living in Russia. She had betrayed her children, he said. Amal remained silent after Bassel said his piece. Something inside her shattered – it was her childish faith in goodness and fairness, her innocence, that went to the dogs in that moment. She stopped believing in any authority, even if that authority was her own father. She couldn't forgive either of their betrayals: her father's cold-blooded lie or her mother's wordless escape. Over the years, Svetlana became nothing but a blurred memory to her.

After her disappearance, Bassel took over the household regime. No one spoke Russian from then on. Bassel was also a man who took food seriously. For a while he even had his own restaurant employing three chefs: one Syrian, one Persian and one Italian. Unfortunately, Amal's father was always quick to lose interest and the restaurant only stayed open for two years. After that he converted it into a French patisserie, then into a small cheese-making workshop and in the end into a bookshop. The chefs became pastry cooks, cheese experts, booksellers. The Italian was the first to escape from Bassel's changing visions – Amal had always loved watching him cook as a child, singing the Internationale with him in Italian. The Syrian chef soon found a new employer too. Only the Persian remained with them, staying part of the family until his death.

Bassel usually came home from work at about seven. Amal had prepared everything by then, the vegetables were peeled and chopped, the herbs washed and the water put on to boil. Amal waited for him in the kitchen in her apron.

Bassel freshened up, watched the news and then started cooking. Amal would help him. Ali stayed in front of the television in the living room, watching films he was too young for. Sometimes he'd come into the kitchen, peek into the pans and beat a hasty retreat. They didn't talk while they worked, but Amal learned when to hand her father a spoon, how to choose the right herbs and deseed a pomegranate.

She was soon making her own tabbouleh and fattoush. Then she tried out the more complicated recipes like mujadara, lentils with bulgur and onions, and *fatteh*, a layered dish made up of fried bread topped with rice, chicken and grilled aubergine, followed by toasted pine kernels and parsley. It was Ali's favourite, so they made it at least once a week.

Lying in bed, Amal smelled spices and onions on her skin and hair, and although the smell didn't necessarily do much for her popularity at school, it helped her to fall asleep at night.

Two years later, Amal's father met a new woman and brought her home with him. There was nothing wrong with her in theory; she was an interior designer from a Druze quarter of Damascus, more sweet than beautiful, small in stature with a very straight nose obtained on a trip to a Teheran beauty clinic. But Amal had the feeling Bassel wanted to overwrite the memory of Svetlana with his new love.

He married a second time. The arguments between Bassel and Amal mounted up – he wanted her to come home earlier, wear longer skirts, not be seen with strange men in public and take better care of the household. Amal spent as much time as possible away from home, constantly looking for ways to provoke Bassel.

Amal's relationship with her father only improved once his second marriage failed.

Hammoudi's parents, both sober and principled people, start suggesting he looks for work. There's no major conversation about it, merely a comment here and there that it would be a shame for him to waste his education, even if it's only until he can leave the country again. Hammoudi feels by turns like the prodigal son and a total loser. He came home to celebrate his future, and now he's moved back into his childhood bedroom.

His parents are scared for him, he knows that, and he knows too that their fear is not due to the political situation but because of his character. It took Hammoudi a long time to decide what he wanted to do with his life. In fact, after leaving school he wanted to do nothing at all; he was more than happy. He enjoyed getting up late, starting the day slowly with a pile of books in bed, with no institution to tell him what to think; long lunches with his mother and epic nights out with his friends. But social decency demanded he learn a profession, no matter how modest. To begin with Hammoudi tried law, but he found the clauses and codes so dry and boring that after two weeks he felt sick even thinking about leaving university. He travelled to Thailand, Laos and China and when he came back he signed up to study Arabic literature. That was another nonstarter. When he dropped out of the course again, his father lost patience and threatened to cut off his allowance. Hammoudi signed up for medicine in the end, without informing his father. They didn't speak for two years, not until Hammoudi had passed his preliminary exams. Then he got a grant from the foreign ministry and continued his degree in France.

Initially, the decision to study medicine had been pure defiance. He wanted to prove to his father that he could manage a degree with no problem at all, and he did. He memorized what he had to know and went through the routine of sitting all the exams. Easy as pie. But during his first student placement in a clinic, he saw the maimed faces of children who'd been in accidents or were born with deformities. It wasn't their appearance that shocked him, it was his own reaction. He couldn't get the idiotic grin off his face while he spoke to the children. Burns victims were the worst. It took him a long time to learn to control himself, and when he at last succeeded he knew instantly he had found his calling, he had finally arrived in real life. He specialized in treating burns victims.

Hammoudi doesn't want to sit around doing nothing in his parents' house any more, so he takes a seat between two filing cabinets in a gloomy office and interviews for a post as a cosmetic surgeon. He doesn't like the job, nor the consultant or the entire hospital. He'd be operating on young women who want their noses fixed – or on their mothers, stubbornly resisting the aging process. Hammoudi doesn't think it would be challenging enough for him. He'd be only too glad to leave it to someone else and he longs for France, for the language in which he can use the precise medical terms and read handwritten medical reports. But his aunts have used their contacts to get him the interview and it would be rude not to attend. Aside from that, he'll soon be broke if he doesn't start working soon, and he couldn't stand the humiliation of asking his parents for money.

During the interview, though, it turns out that Hammoudi isn't even allowed to work in Syria. The consultant on the other side of the desk explains calmly and objectively that he first has to prove he actually studied medicine. Hearing this news, Hammoudi is tempted to laugh out loud. Then the consultant gets up, sends his regards to Hammoudi's aunts and says he's welcome to come back as soon as he's passed his examination.

He has no other option but to go to Damascus and sit the Syrian exam for doctors who studied abroad. At least that will give him a chance to escape his parents' care for a few days. He packs a small bag and sets off for the capital in his father's SUV. He's in an evil mood; he's started smoking again, getting through almost two packs a day, which he now smokes during the eight-hour drive.

This time he stays overnight at the place of a friend, an architect who has several small offices around the city that aren't always in use. One is in the centre of town and has a sofa bed and a bathroom. His friend has left the keys with a neighbour, a young actress who lives on the top floor.

Hammoudi spends a long time looking for a parking space before settling for a spot almost a kilometre away from the apartment. It's cold and Hammoudi thinks about picking up some new clothes while he's in Damascus. Most of his belongings are still in Paris, with Claire. He'd only planned to spend five days in Syria.

The actress is curt when she hands him the keys. She offers him a coffee but her tone implies he'd be better off turning it down. He studies her face; it's attractive, though not all that interesting. Her gaze is absent and she seems irritated. He wonders whether he's seen her in some film or other, and because he's been staring too long he mumbles, embarrassed, 'I think I've seen you in a film.'

'You must be confusing me with someone else,' she answers, and quickly closes the door.

Hammoudi goes down the stairs to his friend's office. The rooms are dark and stuffy but not as uncomfortable as he'd imagined, though they're no match for the Four Seasons. He strips down to his underpants, stretches his tired limbs out on the sofa, writes a text to Claire but doesn't send it, and falls asleep.

The next morning, Hammoudi finds himself alongside four other doctors, two of whom studied in Ukraine, one in Russia and one in Oxford. They are asked questions in a tiny room. The questions are simple but the candidates from Ukraine and Russia have difficulties answering even them. The roaring trade in diplomas and PhDs in the former Eastern Bloc is an open secret. Hammoudi and the Oxford graduate exchange amused glances.

The two of them fail the exam, though. They've been away for too long and have forgotten how the system works, says the false Ukrainian doctor when their names are the only ones missing from the list of passes, and he breaks out in obscene laughter.

Hammoudi stays in his friend's flat for a few more days, waiting for the next examination date, although he doesn't actually want to repeat it. His return to Syria is the greatest defeat of his life, although he can't admit it to himself. During these days, he doesn't know why he should even get up and take a shower in the morning. Once he finally manages to leave the house, he spends hours roaming the streets of Damascus.

On one occasion, he runs into his old friend Reem, a woman from his law course. It's lunchtime so they go to a small Armenian restaurant with a water feature in the courtyard. It's very crowded and Hammoudi has to shout to make himself heard. Reem orders mezze and Hammoudi lamb.

As they wait for their food he tells her about his unfortunate circumstances.

'And they won't let you leave the country?' Reem asks. Hammoudi shakes his head.

'Maybe you could find someone to sort the situation out,' says Reem, though not with much conviction.

'Do you know anyone?'

'I'll ask around.'

'Thank you,' says Hammoudi.

'You know, it's alright living here,' she says after a while, as their food arrives. Hammoudi looks at her and nods.

'Really, it's not bad at all. I don't know what your problem is with the place,' she says, and she lights a cigarette even though they're still eating.

'I don't have a problem with the place,' Hammoudi answers. 'I just want to go back. My girlfriend's in Paris.'

'Then she'll just have to come over here,' says Reem. Hammoudi doesn't look at her, staring instead at the fountain and holding back tears. He feels a hand on his shoulder, Reem tentatively stroking his sleeve.

From then on, old friends keep calling Hammoudi and trying to persuade him that life in Syria isn't all that bad, after all. The conversations exhaust him so much he has to turn off his phone. He distances himself increasingly from all of them – he doesn't want to hear anything about Syria, all he wants is to go back.

One afternoon, he runs into the actress in the semi-dark stairwell. She's wearing sandals despite the cold, and a gold necklace dangles around her neck. She seems confused, though clearly in a better mood than last time. They look at each other without a word, then she gives a faint smile and says hello. Hammoudi nods and is about to pass her when she asks, 'How about a coffee?'

Hammoudi is surprised but he says yes.

Amal asks him up to her flat. The windows are wide open.

'Aren't you cold?' he asks.

'Yes, actually,' says Amal and goes to close the windows. 'Would you like tea?' she asks.

'Okay.'

'Black?'

'Green.'

Amal clatters around with the kettle and then returns to the sofa where Hammoudi is sitting. He takes a surreptitious look around the flat; it's clean but not tidy. Two large, grey sofas face each other in the living room and the walls are decorated with pictures obviously done by art students. On the wide windowsill are potted plants, equally obviously in need of watering.

'Have you moved into the office?' Amal asks.

'I'm only staying a few days.'

'Where are you from?'

'Deir ez-Zor.'

'Ah, a provincial boy,' she says blithely.

'I've been in Paris for the past seven years,' Hammoudi responds, instantly annoyed with himself for trying to impress Amal. Then he adds, 'The city's changed.'

'Deir ez-Zor?'

'Damascus.'

'What do you mean?' asks Amal, studying his face.

'The atmosphere's different, as if something's about to happen. People aren't hiding any more.'

Amal rises to her feet and Hammoudi realizes he's gone too far. She must assume he's with the secret service and wants to quiz her about the silent protests in the city, he thinks. He mumbles something about being tired and makes a quick exit. Amal doesn't try to stop him from leaving.

Hammoudi repeats the exam a few days later. The Oxford graduate is there again too. This time, though, both of them have discreetly placed an envelope on the chairman of the examination board's desk. They don't answer a single question, even when the examiner asks them directly several times. After passing the exam, they part ways swiftly. They're both embarrassed.

Amal is on stage practising a scene for the graduate performance at the Institute of Dramatic Arts. She's tired and hungover and insufficiently prepared. The male lead doesn't know his lines and is sweating profusely. Amal, smelling of powder and chewing gum, shouts at him that she wants a divorce, realizing she's missed her cue. At that very moment, her phone rings. The other student looks genuinely sympathetic, while the professor bestows a scornful glare upon her.

The professor is from Moscow and communicates with the class solely through an interpreter, despite having been married to a Syrian woman for twenty-five years. The perfect target for student jibes, with his eternal plaid shirts and bloodshot eyes. Amal could understand him without the interpreter, but he usually turns up to classes drunk and slurs his words so badly that the interpreter has to make up what to translate.

The professor is responsible for some of the most unpleasant moments during Amal's course, and the fact that she's just filmed a TV series playing the sought-after leading role doesn't make matters any better. Amal earned twenty-thousand euros in cash for the role, an obscene sum of money, especially for a debut. Unfortunately, the professor is about as much a fan of TV series as he is of Amal's acting skills.

Once she's finally managed to turn off her phone, the professor breaks up the rehearsal, shouts for a while and threatens to leave the room. Amal hopes he falls down dead. She asks him if she can leave, at which he gestures with his hands as though trying to shoo away a fly. She quietly curses him, picks up her bag and her script and says goodbye to a few of the other students with kisses on the cheek. She's particularly polite to Rami, who's always slightly inhibited and admitted to her two years ago that he works for the secret service.

She marches out of Wannous Hall, scrabbles around in her bag for her sunglasses and puts them on. Despite being one of the most modern buildings in all of Damascus, the Institute's façade with its staggered white cubes reminds Amal of a once sophisticated holiday resort somewhere on the Crimean Peninsula. The Institute's spacious garden adds to that feeling, with its fig and apricot trees, jasmine bushes, cypresses, planes and poplars grouped around a statue of Hafez al-Assad in a rather odd pose. Amal suppresses the impulse to spit at the monument and hurries past the group of students lounging outside the entrance to the opera house.

The Institute has been admitting increasing numbers of applicants with connections to the secret service or the army. The boys and girls are driven to class in limousines with darkened windows and sit at their desks with loaded but safety-locked weapons, and everyone knows not to criticize them too harshly. That's another reason why Amal wants revolution, wants it absolutely, and so she takes out her phone and calls back the unknown number.

'Do you want to come dancing with us at the Marmar tonight?' asks a male voice on the other end of the line, breaking like a teenager's. It's a voice Amal has never heard before.

'Of course,' she answers quickly.

'We're meeting at seven,' the voice says, and then the line goes dead.

The Marmar never opens before nine but they have to use code words to arrange meeting places for a demonstration.

Amal knows by now that the Marmar stands for the Libyan embassy, because the nightclub is nearby.

Amal buys *kanafeh* on the way home, though she ought not to eat pastries if she wants to keep her figure. Damascus has changed dramatically over the past few weeks. The city is full of secret service men, walking the streets in small groups, checking crowded squares and crossroads and being driven from place to place in white Opel estate cars and buses. Amal automatically crosses the road when she sees one of them, and they're truly impossible to mistake: shaven heads, wide shoulders, eyes hungry for power and luxury. Fear is written on so many faces. They're waiting for the revolution to conquer the city.

Since the demonstrations began in Tunisia, Amal has been studiously learning the language of revolution. She sits at her computer at night watching videos from Egypt, Tunisia and Bahrain, reading everything about the uprisings that for reasons she can't decipher are referred to as the Arab Spring – to be followed by the obligatory long winter. Facebook, the latest drug of choice of Syria's young generation, hosts heated discussions. It's a place to share news, meeting points and information, to argue and debate, and it feels briefly as though anything were possible, as though they really were the people. Syria's young generation feel solidarity with their peers in Tunisia, Egypt and Bahrain, and dream of a just world.

Amal and Luna are standing outside the Libyan embassy with about a hundred others. The sun is setting and the air is growing cooler. The daylight will dwindle rapidly from now on.

Luna stares at the line of policemen opposite them. It looks as though she's trying to memorize every face. A few hours ago, Gaddafi commanded his forces to shoot at demonstrators in Libya, and Amal gives her body the order to stand still.

Luna looks like she's come straight from the beauty salon. Amal wonders what's got into her friend – she normally abhors crowds. She's from a rich family and has three older sisters and two younger brothers, with the result that none of the children are policed all that strictly. Equipped with the requisite parental leniency and a generous allowance, Luna is accustomed to doing only what she feels like and above all *when* she feels like doing it. Toppling the regime wouldn't be in her interests – her father and brothers hold important posts – but Luna can't resist a brief flirt with revolution. It's as though she were trying on a dress she knows she'll never wear; it flatters her figure but shows off too much bare skin. As soon as Luna found out about the demonstration she wanted to come along, at any price.

Amal and Luna's relationship is complicated; they're not just friends, they are also rivals. Luna admires Amal's independence and thinks everything comes a little too easily to her, but at the same time she looks down on her slightly. Amal thinks Luna is spoilt and inconsiderate but she'd still do anything for her. It's a friendship neither of them can evade – they come from the same class, move in the same circles, and above all they both love talking and bitching. They know each other so well that they're always capable of finding each other's scar tissue and either soothing it or reopening old wounds.

Many of the demonstrators are clutching candles and the group is soon singing together. Their faces are expectant and oddly unconcerned. Then a man they know says that latecomers trying to join the demo have had their passports confiscated. As he's speaking he gently touches Amal's elbow. His name is Youssef and he studies directing in the same year as Amal. His skin is tanned and his green eyes are framed by a dense ring of lashes. Amal briefly thinks about flirting with him. But seeing as she only recently separated from her ex-boyfriend because he suggested they get married, and her ex is also at the Institute – his father is a distinguished director, his mother an equally distinguished scriptwriter and his grandfather an even more distinguished party functionary – Amal decides it's too soon for an affair. Which is a shame, she thinks, because she'd like to have sex. She soon loses sight of Youssef.

As the darkness deepens, a security officer from the presidential palace approaches the demonstrators, a man with the body of an athlete and an unsettling air. Politely and with the authority of someone not accustomed to repeating himself, he demands that the crowd disperse. No one leaves the square. Luna whispers to Amal, 'Let's go!' But Amal is still obeying her mental command to stand still.

'We'll stay a bit longer,' she whispers back, not quite knowing where this sudden confidence has come from.

Armed soldiers are waiting in eyeshot. It gets colder and people start jumping up and down almost imperceptibly, warming their clenched fists with their own breath. Isolated stars twinkle their hearts out in the sky and Amal thinks of the Mayakovski poem her mother often used to quote:

> If stars are lit
> does that mean – there is someone who needs it?
> Does that mean – it is essential
> that every evening
> at least one star should ascend
> over the crest of the buildings?

About twenty minutes later, a tanker truck drives up and one of the officers announces through a megaphone that the

demonstrators are to make way because the residents are waiting for their heating-oil delivery. Amal sees the road behind
them being blocked off as hurriedly as possible. The tanker
prevents any of the demonstrators from making an escape.

The lights go out in the buildings around them. In a matter
of minutes, four buses loaded with armed soldiers pull up
outside the embassy. They start photographing the demonstrators and shouting obscenities at them. It's not long before
they attack, at first tentatively, almost gently, but soon they
get a taste for it and grow ever more aggressive. They beat
the demonstrators with sticks, kick them when they're on the
ground, and some of them take out their jack knives.

The time has come to make a run for it – Amal drags Luna
after her as her friend emits a single small scream. A woman is
being beaten up right in front of them, falling at the very first
blow. The soldier kicks her in the stomach, the ribs, the side,
the head. The buttons of her blouse come undone and she lies
there on the ground of Hugo Chavez Street in only jeans and a
grey bra while several secret-service men go on attacking her.
Around her, the demonstrators run to and fro, trying to save
themselves. A young man is beaten up in front of them too.
Out of the corner of her eye, Amal registers that it's Youssef.
Luna and Amal run on as fast as they can. They don't stop until
they reach a quiet side street far from the Libyan embassy.
They're breathing heavily, Luna crouched on the ground and
bursting into tears. Amal's lungs are on the brink of collapse
but she tries not to let it show as she strokes Luna's thick, black
hair. A little later, once they've tidied themselves up and calmed
down, they take a taxi and ride home in silence.

The next day, Amal receives a Facebook message from Youssef, asking if she'd like to go for a drink with him. *Why not?* she writes back. She then spends the rest of the morning with her laptop on her bare thighs, clicking through his Facebook profile. They know each other from the Institute but only vaguely. She looks at his holiday photos, snapshots with friends and family, Youssef sitting at his piano, posters for his first film and a photo of his ex-girlfriend. The laptop gets unpleasantly warm on her legs so she puts it aside and calls Luna. She tells her she's going out with Youssef that evening, so Luna goes online at the same time and clicks though his photos while they talk. A few hours later, Amal starts painting her nails and straightening her hair.

That evening, she waits impatiently for Youssef in Bab Tuma, the Christian quarter. When he eventually shows up she stares at his tall figure without a word. He's ten minutes late and as Amal arrived ten minutes early, she's now freezing cold. Youssef has a black eye and a cut above his eyebrow. A slight drizzle falls on them as they stroll along the narrow roads to the Jewish quarter of Old Damascus, where few Jews live these days. Youssef radiates calm and contentment and is taller than Amal remembers. He's thin and wiry, wearing elegant clothes, has an open face and is extravagant with his laughter. His eyes are dark and slightly tilted. Amal notices how much she enjoys talking to him – and would like to sleep with him even more.

They've now stopped outside a bar opposite the police station, which opens out onto a garden. The grass is strewn with empty beer bottles and plastic bags, and discarded condom wrappers. Youssef gives Amal a questioning look; she shrugs and he holds the door open for her. Inside, it is dark and surprisingly cozy.

'Shall we sit down?' Youssef asks, and Amal looks around for seats. All the tables are occupied.

'Over there,' Youssef points at two free places at the bar. Once they've sat down he takes his time to calmly look at Amal – not just as a potential lover but also as a director with aesthetic demands – and decides she's beautiful. She has a very delicate figure that even a TV screen couldn't make too wide, high cheekbones, full lips slightly improved by a surgeon (though Youssef doesn't know that) and radiant white, straight teeth, the result of regular bleaching sessions. Her eyes are almond shaped and as green as damp moss, her ears small and graced with golden earrings, her hair long.

A bad-tempered barman with gelled-back hair deposits a bowl of peanuts in front of them; Youssef immediately takes a handful. He orders two beers and puts a packet of cigarettes on the bar for Amal to help herself. A cool gust of wind wafts in from the garden. Amal reaches for the cigarettes, brushing against Youssef's hand.

They talk about the Institute, avoiding all political subjects in public. To keep the conversation going, Youssef tells Amal about his grandmother, who fled from Palestine to Damascus in 1948, alone with her four children, and lost both her daughters along the way. Despite detesting her husband, she had another four children with him in the Yarmouk refugee camp. Youssef doesn't tell Amal that his father went to prison twice. Once was because a drunk neighbour fell from his balcony and landed on Youssef's father's car – according to Syrian legislation, the owner of the vehicle was responsible for the accident. The other time because his car was parked in Old Damascus and was run into by a secret service vehicle. Youssef's father never got over the primitive way justice was administered. He died when Youssef was ten. Youssef's mother, too, paid a high price for being born under the rule of the Assad clan. She had to raise three children alone, working day and night and never daring to complain out loud about the injustice done to her and her husband, and she died a year ago of heart failure.

There's a large flatscreen TV in one corner of the dimly lit room, showing footage of Umm Kulthum concerts. As the singer performs her greatest hits, Youssef takes Amal's hand.

She looks him in the eye a little longer than necessary. He strokes the back of her hand and his thumb moves across to the centre of her palm, then he runs his thumb and forefinger along Amal's arm as his mouth approaches hers. Suddenly the energy in the room changes – the waiters bustle to the rear, the owner turns on the light, the TV is switched to Al Jazeera with the volume up. The Egyptian vice-president Omar Suleiman, having swapped his military-intelligence uniform for a stylish blue suit only a week ago, announces in a fittingly slow and stately tone that Mubarak will be stepping down from office. Behind Suleiman looms a dark figure, never introduced during the broadcast.

'It's a bad omen,' says Amal, and Youssef looks concerned. He doesn't let go of her hand. Some of the guests clap and the camera pans onto Tahrir Square, where people start cheering, hands, fists and flags raised to the sky. It's an historic event and it weighs heavily on the room. Youssef kisses Amal on the mouth as the night owls still perched opposite the police station swiftly empty their drinks and rush inside their houses.

Youssef pulls Amal up by her elbow and hurries to get her home too. They don't talk about the kiss; they don't talk at all. The moon is round and yellow. Outside Amal's front door, Youssef seems almost shy. Amal gives him a brief kiss on the cheek and goes quickly inside. Youssef stands still for a minute, then walks back into the night.

Amal tries to wash all thoughts of Youssef out of her hair, first cold and then warm, and then she decides to seduce him – but only if he calls her again.

Meanwhile, Luna has other problems. She's waiting ever more impatiently for her lover to leave his wife and their three children. Luna is only twenty-five but she's been divorced twice already. She married her favourite cousin at the age of sixteen, but sadly the two of them didn't get on. She had a baby at seventeen and was a single parent by the time she came of age. Three years later, she married a second time but her husband showed no interest in her son, so she started looking again.

Hoping to give fortune a helping hand, Luna has decided to use black magic. She found out by chance – so she said – that a well-known magician from the Maghreb was coming to Damascus, and she was lucky enough to get a sought-after appointment. Luna wasn't even particularly superstitious, but the man was very rich and it was better to be safe than sorry.

Dark clouds cover the sky from the east as Amal gets out of the taxi. She's running late because one of her neighbours asked her to look after the keys to his flat and hand them over to a friend of his. She's got a white teddy bear in a plastic bag with her for Luna's son, who's out visiting one of his many cousins. Amal warned Luna off this magician 'nonsense', as she put it, but Luna got her own way as usual.

She lives in a beautifully renovated old building. All the rooms are arranged around a courtyard full of sprawling pot plants crowned by a gigantic satellite dish on the wall. Like most families in Damascus, Luna's is dysfunctional. Her father is a fervent Baathist general, even sporting the obligatory moustache – a magnificent and well-groomed example. He has two passions: parrots and pot plants, which make his house look like a botanical garden. The parrots quote Rumi poems, painstakingly taught to them by Madame General. The general's signature often adorns execution orders.

Luna hasn't told her parents why she's called in the magician; her mother tacitly assumes he's a potential bridegroom and Luna's father hasn't asked.

In the family living room, which is stuffed full of dark furniture, stands a tall, attractive and even blue-eyed man. The only thing spoiling the picture is the back of his head, which is as flat as a pancake. Prince Charming has commanded the lights be turned out and the candles lit. Madame General has just brought a tray of coffee from the kitchen, complete with dates, nuts and baklava. The scent of strong coffee and cardamom pervades the room. Amal takes a cup and introduces herself, but the magician takes not the slightest notice. He is blatantly inspecting the room, stopping for a while by the family photos, including several shots of Luna's father in his general's uniform, family holidays and celebrations. He looks at one of them for a particularly long time, then he writes something on the picture frame with his forefinger and makes his way to the kitchen. Amal watches him moving a glass out of place on its shelf so that it's dangerously close to the edge but she lets him get away with it; her curiosity wins out. The magician placidly lights incense sticks, enough to knock out a large cow. Then he goes back to the living room, takes a seat on the gold-embossed upholstery and announces that a particularly evil djinn is living in the house. He takes Luna's hand and says, 'Someone put something in your food when you were just a child. I see a large, yellow-painted room and a very strong woman who could not have children.' As he speaks he tries to read Luna's face for signs that he's right – although it would be hard to get it wrong, Amal thinks – nearly every house in Syria has a yellow room, and there are infertile or unmarried women in almost every family.

Luna gives a slow nod and the self-proclaimed magician lets go of her hand, which drops loose towards the floor. He now raises his arms to massage his temples with his thumbs, as though clairvoyance was very exhausting. 'There were children of your age sitting around you, and you were eating the Eid meal. There were shaabiyat pastries—.'

'But every Sunni family serves shaabiyat pastries,' Amal butts in, and she notices that one of Luna's rings is missing. Unlike the magician, though, she knows the diamond is a fake.

The man punishes her with a disdainful glance and Luna too gives her a warning look. Just at that moment, something breaks in the kitchen.

'Go and look!' the magician commands Luna's mother. His voice holds an authority to which he's not entitled, which makes it all the more convincing. 'I think the djinn has broken a glass. Probably on the top shelf to the left of the fridge.'

Madame runs straight to the kitchen, shortly followed by a shocked call of *'Ya Allah!'*

Luna looks in her direction, troubled. She doesn't notice the missing ring.

A storm sets in outside, rain and branches whipping against the thin windowpanes. The magician goes on guessing. 'One of your cousins saw it at the time but she didn't say anything.'

'Why not?' Luna asks quietly. Her voice is trembling with agitation.

The man fixes his eyes on her and says, 'She was jealous.'

Fearfully, Luna enquires, 'Of me and Bilal?'

He gives a self-satisfied nod. Now he even has a name. Amal sighs and sits down on the edge of the sofa. The rain is coming down in streams. Several rolls of thunder sound in a row, and shortly afterwards the sky is lit up by delicate lightning flashes.

Luna's mother returns from the kitchen, as pale as death, balancing shards of glass on a dustpan. Her eyes are already flickering with panic. Luna's father comes rushing down from the upper floor. The stairs groan under his weight.

'If you breathe on the photo in the silver frame, a name will appear, and a boy with that name will die within the year,' the magician announces with much ceremony, now blatantly eyeing Luna's body. He stares at her small breasts outlined beneath her yellow dress, at her slim waist and her lips, painted dark red. Amal feels like a voyeur who ought not to be witnessing the scene, but she can't tear herself away.

Luna and her mother instantly jump up to take a look – and a name really does appear on the photo frame: Ali. All eyes turn involuntarily to Amal.

Luna's father shrugs and confirms Amal's thoughts: 'So? There are at least three Alis in every family. Why didn't you just go ahead and write Mohammad on it?' He has a habit of speaking in a barking, military tone at home with his family.

The magician closes his eyes in a theatrical gesture and says at a slightly altered pitch, 'The djinn has put rats' droppings on your marital bed. You will lead no married life until the djinn leaves this place.'

While he talks to Luna and her mother the magician looks them straight in the eye, with the obvious result that they return his gaze and don't notice his hands. He has already slipped the odd thing into his pockets, the ring, a silver spoon here and there. As they now all enter the master bedroom, he surreptitiously flicks a small portion of rats' droppings onto the bed. He's not a bad actor, Amal realizes with respect. Only she and Luna's father saw that the shit came from his direction; for the others, it looked like something supernatural really had taken place. Luna's mother blanches and faints, her husband catching her just in time. That sets off a terrible fit of rage from the general. He lowers his wife's unconscious body from his arms onto the carpet and grabs the magician by the shoulders, shouting that he's a godless man and should get out of his house; he should end up in Saudi Arabia where they have the death penalty for his kind. And he's going to have him locked up and he'll personally ensure he never sees daylight again. He sprays saliva as he yells. His lower lip trembles after every sentence.

His daughter and his wife, who has now recovered her senses, besiege him and beg him to let the magician go.

The general spits on the floor and leaves the room. His opponent acts unimpressed and suggests taking a closer look at Luna's bedroom. Once they get there he grips her by the wrist and presses her gently onto the bed. Her mother is quick-witted enough to follow them, and Amal too hurries after them, not expecting the magician to go that far. Luna's mother sits down on the bed next to her daughter and asks, 'What can we do?'

'Well, there are various options – an amulet would help, of course, there's a shop in the old city where you can get that kind of thing. But that won't be enough. I have a lot of clients from the Gulf States who use more drastic methods. It depends how much you want something, Luna.'

Luna looks at him wide-eyed. She's sitting hunched on her bed, passive and shocked. Her hands are wrapped around her body and now she starts rocking back and forth.

'What kind of options?' her mother asks.

The magician cautiously unbuttons Luna's blouse; Amal doesn't know whether to leave or not. But then she decides to put an end to the whole mess. She puts her hand between the magician's shoulder blades and whispers in his ear, 'That's enough now. If you don't stop I'm going to call the police, and don't forget you're in the home of a general in the Syrian army.'

Amal lives in the centre of Damascus in what is one of the city's tallest buildings, even though it only has four floors. The law doesn't allow structures to be built any higher than the parliament. Her flat is large and luxurious, across two storeys – a gift from her father for passing the entrance exam for the Institute of Dramatic Arts.

Youssef picks Amal up in the evening. They chatted on Facebook earlier and decided to go to a demonstration together.

Youssef's hair is shorter now, Amal notes, and she kisses him despite her plan not to start a new affair. Amal didn't hear anything from him for three days, and even that brief absence was enough to unsettle her.

'I missed you,' Youssef says.

'Is that why you didn't get in touch?'

Youssef says nothing, embarrassed.

'Let's go,' says Amal.

'Are you cross?'

Demonstrations are always held right after Friday prayers. They call it the 'Friday of Dignity'. Every demonstration is given a name, voted on in advance on the internet. But there are also protests more like flash mobs. A dozen activists gather outside a government building and chant demands, then instantly disperse.

Today, about a hundred people are outside the Interior Ministry to demand the release of political prisoners. Their eyes are restless, mistrustful and tired, not a spark of optimism left in them. They hold photos of prisoners, most of them more than a decade old. Many of the young people standing there haven't seen their fathers since they were infants.

Amal and Youssef are in the middle of the protest. Amal shivers even though it's warm, and suddenly she's gripped by utter hopelessness. It's like a dark premonition of things to come. Several people call out *'Selmiyyeh! Selmiyyeh!'* meaning 'peaceful'.

'Let's go, I've got a bad feeling about this,' Youssef says. Amal nods in relief and they leave the square without further discussion. They don't hold hands as they walk side by side but their bodies are so close that there can be no doubt, even for random passers-by.

After walking aimlessly around the city, unsure of how to fill the time before sleeping together, they both look up at the sky, now full of stars. Amal looks for a lighter but can't find one. Youssef holds his out to her.

'Thanks,' says Amal.

The silence grows uncomfortable, the tension increasing.

'Shall we get a drink somewhere?' Amal asks.

Youssef nods, a little disappointed.

They go to a small, crowded bar close to Amal's flat, a place used mainly for buying and selling drugs. The dance floor is small and no one has cleaned it in years.

Youssef pulls Amal onto it anyway. He's not a bad dancer but Amal still thinks a new relationship with someone from the Institute would be a bad idea. After half an hour, he goes to the bar and returns with two glasses. Exhausted, they drop down onto a sofa and their bodies slide closer to one another. There are people coming down from drugs on the floor near the toilet. Youssef and Amal are sipping their drinks through straws when the news comes that the demonstration has been violently broken up, with a number of arrests.

'Shall we go?' Amal asks.

'I'll walk you home,' says Youssef.

Walking towards her house again, Amal tries to remember how tidy she left her flat. As soon as they get there, Youssef takes off his shoes and glances around the living room while Amal switches on lamps and clears away the clothes scattered across the furniture. Youssef stands and looks at her bookshelves to give Amal a little time.

'Is this your mother?' Youssef points at a photo on the top shelf.

'Yes.'

'She's beautiful. Are you very close?'

'The last time I saw her was just before my eleventh birthday.'

Youssef drops the subject.

Amal sits down on the sofa and takes her shoes off too. Her feet are hurting; the straps of her sandals have left bright red marks. Youssef sits down opposite her and massages her feet. She relaxes, closes her eyes and only opens them again when Youssef goes to the bathroom. His breath smells fresh on his return.

'Did you use my toothbrush?' Amal asks.

'My finger,' answers Youssef.

'You can stay,' says Amal.

The next morning, Amal makes pancakes, wafer-thin crêpes served with *labneh* and red caviar. It's mainly Youssef who eats them, Amal content to watch him and drink a large cup of tea.

'I'm going to marry you,' says Youssef.

'But then you'll have to make me breakfast!'

Youssef wakes Amal shortly before four the next morning. It's still dark outside, only the moon and a few stars alight in the sky. They haven't left the flat for more than twenty-four hours.

'What's the matter?' Amal asks, drowsy, and turns on her front.

'Do you want to come? We're doing an action,' Youssef answers.

'What kind of action?'

'No big deal.'

'Then at least have the decency to make us coffee first,' says Amal as she stretches, slowly and clumsily. She's sure she doesn't want to be part of any political 'action', she doesn't even want to go to any more demonstrations, but then she doesn't want anyone to accuse her of not doing her bit; she's said the same too often herself.

Youssef brings her a generously sugared Turkish coffee. Amal mumbles a word of gratitude, even though she can't stand Turkish coffee. She only drinks Italian espresso, which she gets friends to bring from Europe and stores in her freezer. Her visitors always help themselves and use up her supplies, so she keeps a large tin of Turkish coffee next to the stove for them but never uses it herself. She hasn't reached the point of telling Youssef that yet, though.

They drive to a square full of cars not far from the presidential palace, designed by a Japanese architect and bathed in pale blue light. A squat building with marble walls enthroned upon Mount Mezzeh. It resembles a genuine tyrant's palace, cold, dark and above all out of reach.

Youssef stops the car and asks Amal to park it on a side street, where she waits for him with the engine running while he and two friends distribute hundreds of ping-pong balls over the usually busy road. Amal turns on the radio. She ought to be concentrating and alert to every sign of danger, but she's nervous and the music calms her down. Two minutes in, Youssef throws himself onto the passenger seat, slams the door and yells, 'Let's go!' His friends make their own getaway. Amal stalls the car and Youssef slaps his hand on the dashboard. She tries it again and now they drive steadily away from danger.

Later, back in Amal's living room, via several cameras installed by a friend of Youssef's the day before, they watch security men in dark suits and aviator shades chasing after the balls in an attempt to collect them up. Amal laughs long and loud, the first time she's breathed easily since the beginning of the revolution. Youssef and his friends edit a video and upload it onto YouTube. Later, Amal cooks desert truffles brought from Deir ez-Zor by a friend at the institute. She boils them carefully, slices them and standing eats four of them dipped in salt, with Youssef by her side.

The eighteenth of March 2011 is a hot day. The air shimmers with heat and aggression; the sun is at its zenith and beating mercilessly down on thousands of demonstrators pushing their way to the football stadium. The Al-Fotuwa team from Deir ez-Zor was supposed to play against Tishreen today; the team belonging to the president and trained by one of his cousins. But by the time Hammoudi and Naji arrive at the stadium the Al-Fotuwa Ultras have already set light to the other team's bus and two police cars, so the match can't take place as planned.

Not without reason do the Al-Fotuwa Ultras claim to be the worst ultras in the world, worse than the Galatasaray fans. They follow their team everywhere, travelling in dozens of buses made for fifty passengers but each carrying two hundred. They cling onto the roofs and get ready for their 'fun'. Their team's last win was twenty-six years ago.

The worst night in Deir ez-Zor is Friday night, when families wait to find out whether their sons will come home alive; deaths are not uncommon at away games. The fans die either in traffic accidents or knifings. Once they do get home in one piece, the punishment begins. Whole streets band together, with twenty-five fathers lashing out at forty sons, their neighbours all too happy to help out. Hammoudi's brother has often been among the young men beaten on Friday evenings.

Now, though, the throng of football fans has mobilized a demonstration against the regime. Hammoudi marches in their midst, full of conviction; it's the regime that has cheated him out of his own life. Several neighbours pat him on the back; almost all of them are out on the streets. Hammoudi is wearing the team's shirt, enthusiastically loaned by his brother, and is in the midst of the group. There are so many people around him that he can't even make out their separate faces. His muscles are tense and his neck is wet with sweat, but at the same time he feels more alive than he has for a long time. He knows this moment might make him a son of his city. Perhaps for the first time in his life.

Deir ez-Zor is facing a turning point and everyone knows there's no going back now. Hammoudi has caught fire. He chants slogans not dictated by the regime, and it's the first time in the past few months that he decides his own actions. He feels himself regaining control of his life and he never wants to give that up again. Perhaps this is freedom, he says to himself.

A few older men throw their sandals at the blockish, larger-than-life statue of Assad looking down at the masses from the stadium entrance. The sculptor gave the statue a strangely fixed stare more fitting for a drug addict than a president. But power is a drug too. Hammoudi takes a photo of the sculpture to send to Claire later. The young demonstrators follow his lead, taking out their phones and filming each other. They'll upload the material to YouTube later on. Fists are raised, someone yells 'Alahu Akbar!' – 'God is great!' Someone else calls out, 'A curse upon your soul, Hafez!' and then everyone chants together: 'The people demand the end of the regime!' Their anger sparks the same feeling in Hammoudi. He's angry at being subject to the regime's whims, at this country holding him prisoner, at Claire not even being willing to visit him in Syria. At last he can vent that anger.

By the evening there's nothing of it left, only resignation. Hammoudi takes a last look at the photo he took for Claire and deletes it.

Amal drops her bag by the front door as she enters her father's house, kicks off her shoes and throws them over to the bag. Her brother's on the sofa in the living room with a laptop on his thighs, watching Al Jazeera at full volume.

Amal casts a glance at Ali's screen. They're showing footage from Deir ez-Zor. Men dancing in rows, yelling at the tops of their voices and demanding the end of the regime. The commentator's voice cracks with excitement and euphoria.

Ali has the same delicate features as his sister and curly black hair that he keeps short. He's younger but a whole head taller than Amal. When they were smaller and Svetlana had just left them, Ali would crawl into Amal's bed every night and she'd stroke his hair until he fell asleep. She came up with fairy stories for him when he was afraid of the dark and she checked under his bed for monsters. She baked him birthday cakes, she sang for him when their father was on one of his business trips and she read to him from children's books. Later, she was the one who checked his homework and reminded their father it was time to buy new winter shoes for him.

A few years ago, Bassel came into a great deal of money by means of murky deals with the regime and moved into the high-end neighbourhood of Yafour, about forty kilometres west of Damascus near the border to Lebanon. The area is populated mainly by generals, high-ranking officials, thieves and gangsters – people with money and power. Their villas come with swimming pools embedded in lush, green lawns, the walls inside studded with bad but expensive art and stolen archaeological artefacts from Palmyra. The inhabitants protect their possessions with gold Kalashnikovs à la Saddam Hussein. Amal likes coming home nonetheless – she enjoys the luxury and often invites friends to extravagant pool parties on the weekends when her father's away.

She joins her brother on the couch, sinks back into the cushions and drapes a woollen blanket over her feet. It's a large room, the walls decorated with colourised photos of their grandparents, with old books and Bohemian crystal gathering dust behind glass in bulky cabinets. One reminder of their mother's existence is the Red October piano, made in the early sixties and shipped from Leningrad to Syria by complicated means. The piano has been standing proud and lonely in the salon for years, neither used nor tuned. Above it hangs a photo of Amal and Ali's Russian grandmother, a woman with earnest features, hair combed tightly back and large earlobes showing off two fake diamond studs. She survived the Siege of Leningrad, which earned her Bassel's respect. The photo is his only other concession to his children, the only proof of Svetlana's existence.

'Revolution's going to break out,' Ali says without emotion.

Amal tries to read his face but his expression appears absolutely indifferent. She doesn't know what her brother thinks about revolution; there are lots of things she doesn't know about him. Two years ago, he distanced himself from her with the cold cruelty only a teenager can muster.

'Will you make me a coffee?' Amal asks.

'Sure.' Ali gets up and slouches over to the kitchen. Amal picks up her brother's laptop and clicks her way through Facebook. A lot of activists have posted photos and videos of Daraa. Schoolchildren were tortured there for writing critical slogans on walls. Other towns are also staging demonstrations; almost a million people have confirmed their attendance. This time something really big is happening, Amal thinks.

'What shall we make for dinner?' Ali asks. It's an old family tradition – the two of them go to the market every Saturday and then cook together.

'What do you feel like?'

'Fatteh,' Ali answers, as he does every time.

They drive to the souk in the next town. Amal moves at an easy pace along the cool streets and inspects the crates of fruit, vegetables, pistachios and the heaps of spices. The shopkeepers sit on plastic chairs outside their stores, drinking tea and passing prayer beads between their fingers. There are no crisps in Amal's world, no stock cubes or packet sauces, everything is made from scratch. That's why she doesn't like supermarkets; she needs to touch the products and smell them.

Ali walks a pace behind Amal, carrying the shopping. They hear snatches of conversation everywhere they go, almost all of them about Daraa. A photo of the president on the front page of an old newspaper lies crumpled up outside a shop. Ali picks it up carefully, knowing that some of the shopkeepers spy for the secret service and could have him put behind bars for not respecting the photo.

They're back in the kitchen half an hour later. Al Jazeera is still reporting on the demonstrations; they turn the volume down. The small table between them is covered with piles of mint, basil, coriander and parsley on plastic trays. Clumps of earth are still clinging to their roots. They pick the leaves and put them in salt water, then they wash the vegetables and start chopping them, Ali not forgetting to tease his sister as usual as she loses her temper every time her system of different chopping boards for herbs, vegetables, onions, garlic, citrus fruits, fish and meat is messed up. As they work, the voice of the singer Fairuz fills the room. They've had enough of the news.

'Do you remember our mother?' Amal asks suddenly, in the middle of a chorus.

'Barely,' says Ali, adding after a while, 'Why do you ask?'

'No idea.' Amal shrugs and lights a cigarette. 'I've just been thinking about her a lot recently.'

'I can't even remember what she looked like.'

'She was beautiful.'

'Very.'

'And then she left us,' Amal says and puts out her cigarette. A few days ago, she sat at a piano for the first time in years. Her mother had hired several different tutors to come to their house every afternoon and teach Amal piano, music theory and music history, composing and singing. After that Amal had to practise for two hours, with her mother correcting her playing. Amal can't remember why Svetlana was so obsessed with teaching her to play. But when she saw a piano in Youssef's living room she couldn't resist. The piece she played, a Chopin nocturne, sounded awful; her fingers had forgotten their technique.

Bassel deposits his briefcase in the hall, removes his jacket and puts it neatly over a coat hanger on the coat stand. Once tall and slim, Bassel's body is no longer immune to time's passing – his hair has gone grey but at least it hasn't fallen out like most of his contemporaries', his belly has grown soft and visibly convex, and his back is no longer strong and straight. A slipped disc a year ago came as a rude reminder of advancing age.

He notes with satisfaction that the table is laid and the mezze already served. He shuffles into his slippers and goes to the kitchen, where his children are standing side by side at the stove.

'Good evening.' Bassel kisses each of them on the cheeks. 'What are you cooking?' he asks, lifting the saucepan lid as he speaks. Food has always brought him joy. Now he burns his lips on the hot spoon.

Amal wags an admonishing finger at him and laughs.

'Fatteh,' Ali answers, and Bassel nods. Then he pours himself a glass of wine and sits down at the kitchen table. There's a beguiling scent of saffron in the air.

'How are things at the Institute?' he asks Amal.

'Fine,' she says, bored. 'We're rehearsing Wannous.'

'All that stuff about the Palestinians again?' Bassel sighs.

'What else?' Ali comments.

'It's perfect right now – they say there are Israeli agents on the streets stirring up the public,' says Amal, barely able to rein in her excitement. Her cheeks are aglow. She expects her father to agree.

'And I very much hope you two are staying away from the demonstrations.'

Ali and Amal stare at their father.

'You think it's romantic but there's too much at stake, we're not ready for a revolution. We don't have political parties or civil society. Our civil servants are corrupt and ineffective.'

'It can't be stopped now,' says Amal.

Ali listens without comment, crunching on a piece of carrot and waiting for the storm to pass.

Bassel waves his arm to dismiss Amal's words and lowers his voice. 'Oh, yes it can! They mowed everything down in Hama in 1982 and after that no one dared to raise their voice. It'll be just the same this time.' His voice has a touch of irritation to it.

Hama has become a code word, conjuring up memories of the last uprising and intended to curb this one. The Hama rebellion was launched by the Muslim Brotherhood. To consolidate his position in power, Hafez al-Assad sent in the military and had the entire city demolished. People were put up against the wall and shot, raped, thrown out of windows, run over by tanks and slaughtered in the hospitals. This *punishment* went on for three weeks, with entire neighbourhoods reduced to rubble. No one spoke about the events in Hama, no one reported on them, no one documented them. Even today, no one knows exactly how many people were murdered there. But they know what price the regime was prepared to exact to stay in power.

'Society could reorganize itself, on a democratic basis,' Amal says, trying to stand up for her ideas again. 'We could learn.'

'You're too old to be that naïve,' Bassel replies as he lights a cigar. 'And anyway, that's not how I raised you.'

Bassel glares at his daughter with patriarchal fervour. Amal withstands his gaze.

After her rehearsal, Amal finds one hundred and sixty-three calls to her phone from 'caller ID blocked'. When she picks up the one hundred and sixty-fourth call, a rough voice says: 'You whore, do we have to call you a thousand times before you answer?'

Amal hangs up before the man can say anything else. The phone rings again immediately and she slings it against the wall, shattering the casing. She fishes out the remains of the SIM card and flushes it down the toilet. She sends Youssef a warning from her computer and then deletes her Facebook account.

So the secret service has found her. Amal knows she has to act quickly. A few of her friends have already been summoned to interrogations that went on for days. She knows she has to either leave the country or find someone who'll put in a good word for her with the regime. That someone will be expensive, though, and hard to track down.

She goes to her father's office; he's now running a construction company. He values his position and his office, which is in an expensive part of Damascus. Most of all though, he loves hunting down new prestigious building commissions, which is why his children rarely see him these days – or that's how he explains his constant absences. Here in the air-conditioned, sunlit rooms, which have a sense of luxury rather than elegance, the latest addition to the décor is a portrait of Bashar al-Assad. A huge photograph in a heavy, mahogany frame. Amal looks at the picture for a long time. She jumps when her father puts his hand on her back. He smells of cigars and disinfectant.

'I though photos in the office were a distraction?' say Amal, adding, 'At least that's what you always used to say about putting up photos of us.'

'This is different,' Bassel explains coldly as he puts his arm around Amal's shoulder. 'Did you just happen to be passing?'

'I've got a problem.'

He raises his eyebrows and then asks quietly and in Russian, 'Is it something we should discuss outside?'

Amal hasn't heard Bassel speaking Russian since Svetlana's disappearance. She's unsettled by it now and tries to read his expression. Bassel guides her out of the room.

The two of them go down to the garage and get into his car. He turns on the radio and then gestures to Amal to speak. She takes a deep breath and tells him about the phone calls.

'You're going to get a summons,' says Bassel.

'I know,' says Amal.

A few days later, Bassel has chased down a high-ranking government official with whom he studied in Moscow. In return for a generous sum, he is to get hold of a secret-service officer to make sure nothing happens to Amal in the event of her being summoned.

A week later, Amal receives a message on her new prepaid phone from 'caller ID blocked', instructing her to report to the Air Force Security Service headquarters the next morning. That same day, Bassel hands the official an envelope stuffed full of dollar bills, in exchange for the promise that Amal won't be arrested.

The Damascus headquarters are known as the 'Holocaust'. There are several secret services, in fact, and each of them has at least one branch office in every part of every town, down to the tiniest village in the country.

A roadblock has been set up outside the entrance. Several police cars and a tank flying a small Syrian flag guard the building. The tiny forecourt is made of concrete, the high walls wrapped in barbed wire. Masked guards cradle primed machine guns on every corner, and the various men in grey suits with guns slung loose around their hips are impossible to overlook.

A young soldier leads Amal and her advocate along endless corridors with tattered carpet and yellowed wallpaper. The walls are dotted with identical portraits of Bashar al-Assad. The soldier rushes ahead so fast that Amal has trouble keeping up with him without breaking into a jog.

In the end he stops outside a solid iron door. It creaks loudly when he opens it with some effort. Inside the general's office, where power reaches its zenith, a deathly silence reigns. An unpleasant smell has lodged itself in the upholstery. There are no photographs of the president here, not even behind the general's desk. He now clears his throat for the first time. At that very moment, Amal feels an irrepressible need to go to the toilet. The advocate has left the room again in response to a gesture Amal wasn't able to interpret.

'Were you at the demonstration outside the Libyan embassy?' the general asks through his huge moustache, with no pretence of an introduction. He stands there with his legs apart and his belly extended, puffing greedily on a cigar. The smoke quickly fills the small room.

Amal is suddenly reminded of how her mother used to say the size of a man's moustache was a measure of how often he hit his wife.

'Yes, I was,' Amal answers.

'Why?' His eyes wander to her long fingers, bearing neither wedding nor engagement ring. 'Has Gaddafi done anything to you?'

'I thought it was authorized.'

'Who gave you permission to think?' The general looks her firmly in the eye and Amal tries not to evade his stare. 'How did you get the idea the demonstration might be authorized?'

'Because so many people posted it on Facebook. I thought it couldn't be illegal.'

'Well, we all make mistakes. I won't hold it against you. What happened then?'

'The demo was broken up,' says Amal, pressing her thighs together.

'And then?'

'I went home.'

'But before that you went to another demonstration, didn't you?' The general doesn't wait for her response, instead opening up an outmoded laptop on his desk and playing a video for Amal, showing her holding a banner and singing a revolutionary song, clearly recognizable. The general has a slight air of a boa constrictor about him.

'Did you take a wrong turn on your way home?' he bellows.

'I was on my way back from the other demo and I happened to see this one. It was on my way home.' Amal shrugs and tries to keep her voice free of any emotion.

'Aha.' The general raises his left eyebrow without further comment and then plays another two videos of Amal demonstrating.

Amal says nothing and neither does the general. His face is only inches away from hers. His eyes are bloodshot and his chin trembles. Amal has the feeling saliva will start running down the trembling spot any minute now. She smells his cigar and his aftershave, which must consist of a combination of heavy woody notes and cheap alcohol, and beneath that she smells vodka. After a while he says, 'Young lady, there's one thing you have to understand. We're not going anywhere, even if Bashar goes away. We're staying. For ever. And if we have to, we won't just burn your kind, we'll burn down the whole country. And now go, and tell your little friends their child's play won't get them anywhere. Tell them we're staying. *For ever*.'

He calms down again and makes a note in large, childish handwriting on shiny paper headed with the words 'Arabic Republic of Syria, Air Force Security Service Department'. Then he dismisses Amal. She now has a file.

Hammoudi orders kebab and a large portion of rice – the revolution makes him hungry. The owner brings his food over in person. Her hair is blonde and elaborately curled, the skin around her eyes and the corners of her mouth sown with fine wrinkles, her lips full and neatly painted. Her eyes are brown and warm and as she puts the blue plate with Hammoudi's squarely arranged food on the table, it's as though her whole body were flirting with him. She spent ten years married to a deeply patriarchal man before he died of a heart attack last year. Rumour has it his death might actually have had other causes.

'Enjoy your meal,' she says, smoothing her dress over her hips.

Hammoudi nods his thanks and reaches out for the cutlery. The meat is juicy and he can clearly taste the rosemary, although the rice is a little plain. He washes it down with Coke. Underneath his bill, he finds a piece of paper with a hurriedly scribbled address, a time of day and a name – Samira.

More out of curiosity than lust, Hammoudi finds himself outside Samira's front door at the arranged hour. As she opens up she clicks her tongue suggestively. A loose dress flatters her figure.

In the hall, an embarrassed Hammoudi takes off his trainers. Samira asks him if he'd like a coffee and signals for him to sit down on the sofa. The room has seen better days – the ceiling is low and bears the brownish cloud formation of past water damage. The windows are covered by heavy curtains.

The electric light is dimmed, the furniture worn and even the family photos – Samira in various poses, usually beaming and surrounded by several children; one picture of her arm in arm with a corpulent man – must have been taken more than a decade ago. Hammoudi would like to ask about the man but he refrains.

She returns a few minutes later with a small tray holding two cups of coffee. How can a person signal neediness and confidence at the same time, Hammoudi wonders.

'Thank you,' he says.

Samira lowers her eyes coquettishly. It's been a long time since Hammoudi slept with a woman. Samira takes his hands and puts them on her hips. As he runs his hands up to her waist, she closes her eyes and backs expertly onto the sofa. Hammoudi suddenly feels infinitely lonely. The sex is mechanical. Once it's over he lies down next to Samira but the sofa is too small for them both. Samira gets up and goes to the bathroom, and Hammoudi soon hears the shower running. He pulls on his trousers and sneaks out of the flat.

After he leaves Samira's house he's plagued by a guilty conscience, despite not having heard from Claire in ages. Both of them have grown increasingly taciturn over the past few months, gradually reducing their contact. It's clear their relationship is over but still Hammoudi wishes he'd found the courage to talk openly to Claire. He's shocked at how quickly they've drifted apart.

The demonstrators want to march through Old Damascus, starting from the majestic Umayyad Mosque and ending at the bustling Marjeh Square, with its hotels and restaurants and the incredibly ugly bronze pillar wrapped in wires, meant to commemorate the first telegraph connection to Mecca. As if it were that easy to get hold of God, Amal thinks, and takes the SIM card out of her phone to be on the safe side. She's decided to keep protesting despite the secret service's warning, and she's far from the only one. Regardless of the arrests, the tear gas, the snipers, the *shabiha* militiamen stabbing or beating demonstrators, more people come to the marches every time. Their revolution is becoming the only conceivable solution.

A few metres away from Amal, a woman is marching in a bright white blouse, black jeans and a white headscarf, filming the demonstration on a handheld camcorder. She turns briefly to Amal, their eyes meet and then she falls to the ground. Amal thinks at first she's stumbled and she takes a step towards her to help. But then she sees the woman's blouse colouring dark red and she kneels down beside her. The woman gasps for breath, no longer sounding human. Blood is spilling out everywhere, from her mouth and nostrils, an absurd amount of blood. It sticks to Amal's hands, clothes, shoes. A young man calls the woman *habibi*, darling, and tells her to stay awake. Amal props her up so she can spit out the blood. Her eyes roll, her right arm twitches, she loses even more blood, and then her eyes suddenly turn inwards, their light extinguished. Her body is still warm. Amal is overcome by a feeling of absolute pointless-ness. She abandons the lifeless body to the crowd now gathered around her and leaves. She doesn't walk, she runs, not even thinking about where she's going – as long as she gets away.

At the next crossroads, two men grab her by the hands. She has no time to react to their assault as she feels a hard jab at her back. Searing pain instantly floods across her lower back and down her legs. Then the leather truncheon descends on the back of her knees. Amal collapses onto the ground. Her cheek hits the dirty paving stone. Another blow. She stays down, curling up and gasping for breath. Then she lifts her arm to protect her head. The men laugh, grab her beneath the armpits and drag her to a white Opel Omega Estate, where they bind her hands with a cable tie and lock her in the boot behind a dividing grille. Although the engine's running, the car is empty apart from the driver, who immediately begins screaming the most vulgar insults at Amal. Up to now, Amal didn't even know most of them existed in Arabic.

Over the next quarter of an hour, four more women are thrown into the boot. They can hardly breathe, let alone move. They feel the pressure of one another's bodies. Now three shabiha men get into the car and one of them turns straight to the women and starts administering electric shocks with a taser. He's tall and muscular, his face relaxed. He enjoys the procedure the same way he'd enjoy swimming in the sea or eating pistachio ice cream. He aims the taser at the same part of the body every time. The pain swiftly becomes unbearable; Amal hears herself whimpering.

The car speeds through Old Damascus. An air freshener tree with the scent of 'new car' sways to and fro above the dashboard. The owner of the taser describes in great detail a group rape, getting the driver so turned on that he stops looking at the street, his eyes fixed on the rear-view mirror. This man is stocky and bullish, with a fat neck. When he turns around suddenly, the man in the passenger seat grabs the steering wheel and yells, 'A curse on the cunt you crawled out of, are you trying to kill us all? Don't you think three men are enough to deal with these whores? Stick to driving before we all die!' He slaps him around the head and the other shabiha men hit out even harder, as if to prove they really have got the women under control.

The car brakes abruptly and Amal is thrown against the grille. One after another, the women are dragged out with their tops pulled over their heads. The worst thing for Amal isn't the pain, it's the humiliation of standing somewhere in the streets of Damascus with her body exposed.

Kicks and punches drive the women on. They're taken to some branch office of the secret service; the prisoners aren't supposed to know where they are, which is why Amal's top is still over her head and her hands are still tied behind her back. She shivers and shakes, although the temperature inside the building is subtropical. Amal feels a hot, rough hand on her ribs and smells a sour, solid body next to hers. More hands grab at her waist; she tries to evade their grip but she can't; someone holds her in place from behind. Now someone kneads Amal's breasts like a butcher clutching a piece of cheap meat, tuts and suddenly throws her against a wall. As she recovers consciousness she's being pulled up, her top is torn off her head and she herself is driven semi naked down a long corridor by blows from sticks, chairs and belts. Fluorescent lights hang from the ceiling, mercilessly illuminating the corridors. People are chained to pipes on either side, many of them no longer conscious. They lie closely packed like cobblestones. Their bodies are strewn with deep wounds, their clothes and skin covered in blood, some faces no longer recognizable. It smells of urine and faeces and screams sound out from all sides.

A bullish man orders Amal to beat the bodies lying on the ground. Amal shakes her head. She can't do it.

'You don't want to, you whore? You think you're something special? Just wait, I'll show you how to do it!' the man yells and shoves Amal aside. The baton in his right hand lands repeatedly on the back of a young man standing in the corridor, leaving red welts. The man screams. His face is a mass of raw flesh, his eyes so swollen they're barely recognizable as such. Amal realizes she's crying.

'Still don't want to?' The guard is in full stride now, his voice getting hoarse.

Amal refuses again and the man starts beating the man hard on the stomach. His victim now utters only an animal moan. Amal can't take any more and calls out, 'I'll do it!'

The guard grins and hands the stick to Amal. She tries to hit the man as gently as possible but she's still hitting him, and she's disgusted with herself.

Minutes later, Amal is shoved into a cell. The space measures two by three metres and holds some twenty-five women. There's a hole in the floor that functions as a toilet. For fear of rats, the women let the flush run all the time, although flush is an exaggeration – it's nothing but a hose with water trickling out of it. The building has never been ventilated. There's no room to lie down; the women take turns to sleep. Two of them step aside to let Amal rest for a while.

One of them kneels down to her and says, 'You've survived the worst, the worst thing is the drive here.' But Amal knows that's not true. She knows everything depends on the secret service's goodwill. She knows only her father and his money can help her, but he warned her he'd need to find out about her arrest in order to save her. Amal's only hope is that one of the officers will call her father and ask for money, and that she'll still be alive by then. Suddenly she collapses. She can hardly breathe, she retches and whimpers and can't stop. The women don't try to help her – they have more important things on their mind: their own survival.

They aren't tortured but they can see through a hole in the wall, presumably made deliberately, as the men in the next cell are beaten. Amal trembles at their screams. The bright fluorescent light is left on at night and she soon loses all track of time. None of the women has been charged with any crime, some are only here because of a picture on their phones, others because their fathers and brothers have been languishing in Syrian jails for decades.

The next morning, Amal and half a dozen other women get their hands and eyes bound. They are shoved into the yard and the security officers order them to say their last prayer before their deaths. Amal sees nothing but the dark fabric of her blindfold; an icy wind brushes against her bare shoulders and knees but she doesn't feel the cold. Some of the women beg for their lives, others are already speaking the *shahada*, testifying to their Islamic faith, and then they are forced to stand in a line. Amal is shoved roughly into the right position by someone who smells of cold sweat and oud incense. The shabiha men load their weapons and fire. They laugh and someone from the group of condemned women joins in the laughter. Amal thinks they shot up in the air. She wants to believe that, very much so. She hears no screams of pain, at least, and doesn't smell blood either. The men load their weapons again and pull the triggers. Once the shots have been fired, Amal tries to ascertain whether she's still alive. Then she tries to locate any pain, mentally scanning her toes and her feet up to her calves, knees, thighs, hips, belly, ribs, chest, shoulders, upper arm, lower arm, fingers, to the other arm, shoulders, neck and up to the top of her head. She decides she must be unhurt. She doesn't know whether the soldiers fired in the air or executed someone next to her; she can hardly remember the faces of the women she was incarcerated with. She doesn't know whether she's still alive by chance or there's some kind of deliberate plan behind it. The weapons are loaded again, shots fired. Amal's blindfold isn't removed until she's back in the cell. When the officers let go of her she staggers.

Three days later, they let Amal go. The sky is clear and cloudless. Birds are singing, people are out shopping, on their way to work, taking their children to school. She feels nothing but the shuddering of her legs, and she looks no one in the eye as she makes her way home barefoot. It's a three-kilometre walk. Amal was only three kilometres away from home. The city's sounds are horribly loud, their echo pulsing against her temples. She keeps getting dizzy and having to lean against walls. Passers-by keep well away from her.

'Good morning,' says Youssef. He's standing outside Amal's front door, wanting to come in.

Amal has a blanket over her shoulders. Her body is strewn with bruises. Her cheeks and arms are covered in scrapes and her feet look like they belong to a vagrant. Her face resembles a desolate landscape. Her head aches. The pain returns at ever shorter intervals and unfurls anew with a fresh force that seems to know no mercy.

'Please let me in,' Youssef says gently.

She carefully unlatches the door chain and takes a tiny step aside so that Youssef can come in. He looks at her, uncertain what to do, then reaches a hand out to stroke her back, but she forbids him from touching her. He's clutching a bunch of flowers. Amal looks at them and bursts into tears; loud sobs that seem never to stop and eventually give way to a throaty staccato. Youssef tries to embrace her but she pushes him roughly away and goes into the living room. Youssef follows her.

'I know where you were,' he whispers in Amal's ear.

'Go away,' Amal manages to press out between sobs, and she doesn't recognize her own voice as she says it.

Youssef longs to hug her. She doesn't move.

'It'll pass,' Youssef whispers.

Amal runs out of the room and locks herself in her pink-tiled, perfectly clean bathroom, leaving Youssef pale and alone. He knocks cautiously at the door but she doesn't react. He sits down on the floor and waits in silence. He spends two hours there.

Once Youssef has finally left, Amal emerges from the bath-room. She throws the flowers in the bin and unplugs her landline, then she switches her mobile to silent and her door-bell off. She's full of unsaid words and she knows she'll never speak them, not as long as Bashar al-Assad and his accursed family are in power. She prowls around her flat, not finding anywhere to settle down, not on the sofa, not in the kitchen and certainly not on the veranda. She can't call anyone because her phone is definitely being monitored, and she doesn't dare to go out. She closes all the windows and draws the curtains. The only light she can bear is a tiny nightlight.

Late that evening, Luna opens the door with the spare key that Amal gave her for emergencies. She couldn't get hold of Amal while she was in prison, so she began to worry. A few days ago, she decided to go to Amal's flat. Since then she's been there regularly, sitting in the kitchen for a while, gazing out of the window, checking her emails and daydreaming about her lover, who still hasn't left his wife.

Luna sits down on the couch next to Amal with two steam-ing cups of tea. When Amal continues staring into space after drinking hers, Luna tries to inject some enthusiasm into her voice and says cheerfully, 'I'm hungry.'

'I've got no food in the house,' Amal answers, devoid of all emotion.

'Shall I order something?'

Amal shakes her head. A little later she's in the kitchen kneading dough while Luna flicks through an Italian *Vogue,* not letting her friend out of her sight. The worktop is covered in flour, sugar and crumbs, open containers of date syrup, rose-water, honey and rose petals everywhere. It smells of melted butter and a heavy sweetness that wipes away all thoughts. The oven is hot, two baking sheets are cooling on the floor and two more are waiting their turn. Amal's gaze is turned inwards, rejecting any contact. Luna has given up trying to draw her into conversation and opened a bottle of whisky instead, which is rapidly emptying. But Amal is very aware that Luna hasn't even asked where she's been for the past few days, and suddenly she's not sure whether Luna is simply afraid to ask or if she thinks she deserved it.

Two hours later, Amal and Luna have their feet up on the coffee table, in front of them a huge, porcelain platter of sticky sweets, which they put silently and methodically in their mouths, one after another, until Amal jumps up, very pale, and rushes to the toilet. Luna runs after her and holds Amal's hair away from her burning-hot face as she vomits.

Every day, people are buried in white shrouds. Facebook and YouTube are flooded with videos of the dying and the dead and their grieving parents. The state TV stations repeat the tale of alleged terrorists and show images of martyrs who died for Assad's glory. The West does nothing, still nothing.

Via his brother Naji, Hammoudi has made contact with the opposition. They try to meet regularly and exchange news on the events in Deir ez-Zor. One of them is a young doctor, Mariam, who says the secret service is now monitoring casualty departments. If demonstrators are admitted, she says, the hospital directors tell them not to treat them; if they do, the doctors are shot.

Hammoudi suspects the revolution has failed. There will be no new Syria. Something terrible will take its place, and yet he still feels better. These meetings have saved Hammoudi; he no longer feels isolated and he can finally forget Claire for a while. For the first time he can really make a difference. At least that's how it feels. And that's why he agrees to break into a hospital to gather evidence of the regime's crimes. They'll be sent on to international newspapers; the reports from Syria are now so appalling that they come across as implausible.

He wants to see the demonstrators' dead bodies before the military police dispose of them. He knows from Mariam that the secret service tortures detainees on the top floors, but no one can get up there without being arrested first.

Hammoudi puts on a doctor's coat, walks into the Al-Noor Hospital and through the casualty department without alerting attention, then takes the lift to Pathology. He's scared, his fingers are clammy but he keeps going; keeping going is all he has left.

The refrigeration units are overcrowded, meaning many corpses are still in the middle of the sparsely lit room. Hammoudi tries not to breathe in but the stench is overpowering. The murdered bodies are littered with traces of torture: burns and bruises, skin cauterized by chemical substances, deep cuts, welts from electric cables, blood still barely congealed. One body is missing its left eye; Hammoudi sees it must have been ripped out. Others have had limbs amputated and teeth kicked in.

Hammoudi feels a sudden hand on his back. He turns around slowly. Behind him is the consultant from the interview he had a while ago. He has suntanned skin, a high forehead and a bald pate. He says nothing, the two of them merely contemplating the bodies in silence through their glasses.

After a while that feels like an eternity but is only thirty seconds long, the consultant says, 'The only thing I can do for you is not report you. Take your jacket and go straight home. Make sure the military don't see you.'

The windows are open, fresh air and the scent of jasmine flooding into the room. The distant sounds of traffic, voices and car horns make Amal feel alive. It has always taken her a long time to get up in the morning, and now she turns on her front in slow motion and then onto her back, like a lumbering beetle, and stretches her limbs. She pulls herself together and gets up.

With a silk dressing gown over her nightclothes, she gets her Italian coffee out of the freezer, makes an espresso in a pot also imported from Italy and pads onto her veranda with her coffee cup. Out there, she encounters a tall man in a balaclava and full martial gear. The man is calmly smoking a cigarette on her property, looking into the distance. He has already set up his long-barrelled sniper's rifle, aimed at the busy square opposite her building.

When the sniper notices Amal he wishes her a good morning with a broad grin that comes across as insolent. He has a friendly round face and the morning really is extremely sunny.

Amal nods at him and asks, 'Has something happened?'

'No.'

'Aha.' Four more snipers are positioning themselves on Amal's roof and the neighbours' roofs look like they're crawling with cockroaches in some kind of biblical plague. She gives the man on her veranda a questioning look. He stares back, extinguishes his cigarette on her floor and fishes a piece of chewing gum out of his pocket.

'Will you be here long?' Amal asks.

'We don't know, but it would be nice if we could use your

toilet. I'll make sure nothing gets stolen.' His voice is friendly, almost apologetic.

'Yes, of course,' Amal murmurs and hurries into her bedroom, where she draws the curtains and gets dressed. Then she starts pacing to and fro. When she notices how ridiculous her behaviour is, she stuffs all the cash and jewellery she has at home into a handbag and leaves the flat in a rush.

Youssef comes to the door half naked, his hair a mess and his eyes still red from the shower. He's clearly surprised to see Amal; they haven't spoken since the bathroom incident. Amal shakes her head in response to his unspoken question and they embrace. She goes into his flat, throws her jacket onto a chair and her high-heeled sandals into a corner. Now it's Youssef's turn to tidy up, relocating an impressive collection of used coffee cups into the kitchen.

They spend the day listening to old records and drinking bad Lebanese wine, until at some point there's a Twitter announcement that Bashar al-Assad is going to give a speech to parliament.

'He's not going to step down,' Amal says.

'Of course not, but he could at least apologize for the crimes in Daraa.'

'Or fire his cousin.'

'Not a bad idea,' says Youssef.

'Now I know why they sequestered my terrace, at least.'

They sit down in front of the TV. It's an old model with a convex rear and random colours on the screen. Bashar al-Assad talks for a long time and yet says nothing, or at least he doesn't utter a word about the revolution or Daraa. Instead, he talks about a conspiracy targeting Syria as a whole. Every now and then he laughs at his own jokes. At the end of his speech, a parliamentarian leaps up with a mildly insane expression on his face and announces that Bashar should rule not only Syria, but ideally the whole world.

Youssef throws an ashtray at the wall. The bulky, crystal dish shatters into hundreds of small crystals and Youssef yells that the president should curl up and die.

'I never liked that ashtray,' says Amal.

Youssef doesn't react, instead launching into a tirade of curses against the president, his father, mother, brothers, uncles and wife.

'It's no use cursing! The neighbours will hear you!' says Amal.

'Fuck the neighbours!' Youssef yells, albeit at a slightly lower volume.

'Pour me a drink instead, or don't you give a shit about me either?'

Youssef glares at her but at least he stops talking.

'I want to have a party,' Amal says after a long pause.

Youssef raises an eyebrow and then laughs out loud. 'I've got a feeling it might be the last one,' he says thoughtfully, once he's finished laughing. 'When, then?'

'Tomorrow.'

Amal gathers her hair up in a bun, smokes one last cigarette, puts on an apron and starts work. It's going to be a huge feast for more than forty guests. Amal has a lot of friends, perhaps so that she doesn't have to get close to anyone in particular. Her kitchen is spacious and open-plan, with large white cupboards, a granite worktop and a kitchen island where her shopping is lined up in countless plastic bags: thin crispy flatbreads typical of Damascus, large tubs of yoghurt, labneh and tahini, pine kernels and walnuts, fresh herbs, whole chickens, a leg of lamb, a small sack of rice, piles and piles of fruit and vegetables, two gigantic watermelons.

Youssef is sitting at the kitchen table with his legs crossed, flicking through Amal's collection of Persian and Arabic cookbooks and waiting for her instructions. Amal mixes a yoghurt and tahini marinade for the lamb, which she then puts in the oven; she fries aubergines and the flatbreads, layering them in her favourite blue bowl with chickpeas and yoghurt and tahini to make fatteh, removes a portion of stock from the freezer and uses it as a basis for *frike*; she makes *fattoush* by frying more flatbread, washing and chopping herbs and vegetables and mixing it all into a salad; she purees chickpeas for hummus, adding tahini, salt, lemon juice and a little garlic. While Amal cooks she forgets Bashar al-Assad, the revolution and the prison, torture and Syria; forgets they exist. She even smiles at Youssef.

Youssef watches her slender hands working, her face concentrated and her forehead damp with beads of sweat. Once the mezze are done she moves on to the Persian main courses, which she only prepares for special occasions. She gets Youssef to chop the herbs and vegetables while she puts fine threads of saffron in a small bowl, pours boiling water over them, covers the bowl with a saucer and sets it aside, then washes the rice and melts the butter. She makes *khoresht-e fesenjan*, a stew of chicken, pomegranate syrup, ground walnuts, turmeric, salt, pepper, paprika, ginger, cinnamon, nutmeg and cloves. Plus another kind of *khoresht* with tender veal and large amounts of parsley, fenugreek, wild leek and dried limes, also stewed for hours. The dishes are served with simple saffron rice and sour cherries.

The scent of cooking fills the whole building. Now Amal takes her shortcrust pastry out of the freezer, bakes it blind for the tarte au chocolat, melts the dark chocolate with cream and a little butter, squeezes lemons for the tarte au citron, then whips egg white for the pavlova, which Youssef is allowed to decorate with fresh berries later, under close supervision.

Amal finishes shortly before the guests arrive. She asks Youssef to open all the windows while she takes a shower. The table is covered with small mezze plates and the heavy cast-iron pans Amal brought specially from France. The air smells of cardamom and cinnamon, of anise, saffron, cloves, sumac and cumin. The scent of the spices and steaming dishes mingles with that of the fresh flowers Youssef brought along – jasmine and of course Damascene roses.

Youssef follows Amal to the threshold of the bathroom and knocks cautiously. She lets him in and opens the shower cabin door. Warm water pelts down on her damaged body and Youssef looks at her, looks closely and studies her bruises, the scraped skin and the prison now inscribed upon Amal's body, and then Amal pulls him close and he buries his lips in the nape of her neck.

At the end of the meal, the guests dunk scraps of bread in the emptying dishes to get at the very last remains, the empty arak bottles crowd each other out and belt buckles are loosened. The evening has been extravagant but not nearly as out of hand as the parties in the months and years before. It seemed as though the guests were just looking for an opportunity to argue, but the rich food calmed their tempers.

Amal has been in bed for some time, with Youssef by her side – Luna has generously taken over the hostess's duties for the rest of the evening. She's in a magnificent mood because her lover has finally moved out of the apartment he shared with his wife and children.

In bed, Youssef strokes Amal's hair and whispers in her ear that he's joined the resistance. He won't be fighting, he tells her, but he is smuggling medicine, bandages and food to the front, where their former fellow students and friends are fighting Assad's troops.

'Promise me you won't fight,' Amal says.

'Am I that important to you?'

'I don't want our revolution to fail,' Amal answers after a while.

Two doctors, a veterinarian, a pharmacist and two nurses are sitting on cushions. Hammoudi and Mariam contacted them because they had seen them at demonstrations, so knew they could count on their support for the revolution. Mariam passes between them with a tray of tea and pastries. Hammoudi admires Mariam's slim figure and her blue eyes, rather like sapphires. She smells of flowery perfume and generously applied oud, a scent Hammoudi never could resist. The curtains are drawn.

Hammoudi is the first to speak, starting by thanking Mariam for letting them use her flat and then everyone else for coming. He feels insecure about the meeting; he thinks he's the wrong person for the job because he spent the past few years outside of Syria, but the others are so warm and affectionate that he soon forgets his concern. He tells them he's planning to set up a secret field hospital.

The pharmacist, a woman with a grey headscarf and dark eyes, says, 'It's getting worse and worse. When doctors, ambulance staff and nurses try to help injured demonstrators they're treated like criminals. They're risking their lives.'

'Someone was shot dead at a checkpoint the other day just because he had painkillers with him,' says a dentist, a chain-smoking man in a navy-blue suit that can't hide his spindly figure.

'I can't imagine that,' says Mariam.

'They'd never go that far!' the vet next to her agrees.

'We have come that far,' the nurse says.

'We have to get organized,' Hammoudi says. 'We could distribute medical kits all over the city. That would be a start, and when a demonstrator is injured a nearby doctor could be informed via a telephone list. That way we'd minimize the risk.'

'Right,' the pharmacist nods. 'I'll take care of the medical kits.'

'We need blood,' says the head of the municipal hospital's orthopaedic department. Hammoudi looks puzzled so she adds, 'The central blood bank is under government control and no blood is "wasted" on demonstrators.'

The vet adds, 'We could import empty blood bags from Iraq. Then catalogue telephone numbers and blood groups of potential donors – if someone needs a transfusion, we can call the people with the right blood group on the spot.'

'We won't be able to test the blood,' Hammoudi points out.

Mariam switches on the ceiling fan; it hums quietly.

'I'm afraid we'll just have to trust people. Anyone with doubts about their health would be better off not donating.'

'We could start with ourselves,' Hammoudi says.

'The most important question of course is how long it will all last. Even if we manage to drum up enough donors we won't hold out for long. It's impossible to set up a whole underground hospital. We'll only be able to treat the mildest injuries,' says the pharmacist.

'It's going to get even worse,' the dentist replies, lighting another cigarette.

'I think so too.'

'I'm afraid the city's going to end up under siege,' the nurse sighs.

Over the next few weeks, they manage to set up a store of medications and medical equipment. Each of them secretly sets aside antibiotics and bandages. They get hold of lighter equipment such as operating lights and surgical instruments, even a small X-ray machine and a generator. Everything is privately funded, which means their supplies are modest. They'll last a month, two at the most. No one is expecting the siege to go on longer than that anyway. Hammoudi works day and night, finally forgetting how much he misses Claire.

Hammoudi and Naji take a walk around town and Deir ez-Zor puts on a fine show for them: the temperature is mild, the evening sun a mere orange-tinted memory against a milky blue sky. They leave the main street, crowded with trucks and minibuses, walk along narrow roads to the suspension bridge and cross it. Families stroll across it in the opposite direction.

On the other side of the river, Hammoudi spots a bird on the dusty asphalt. Its plumage has taken on the colour of sand. It tries to fly away but it seems to have forgotten the right sequence of movements. Hammoudi hesitates to touch it.

'It's not going to make it,' he judges.

'Shall I?' asks Naji, squatting down next to the bird. He puts his hand over the bird's head, Hammoudi turns away, and when he looks back the bird is no longer moving. Naji wipes his hands on a tissue.

By the time the brothers reach the Sahara restaurant, darkness has settled. They are led to a small wooden table. The room is rather grubby, the menu uninspiring. The other guests are families with small children and the children gaze with eyes alight towards a side room hidden from view by a curtain. That room is the real reason for the restaurant's popularity – it's where the animals are kept: a German shepherd, a monkey, a peacock, a hyena, a donkey and a rather stunted lion that is carted around the neighbouring villages in its cage on high days and holidays. It costs five Syrian lira to look at the lion. As children, Naji and Hammoudi were always nagging their parents to come here. Today they're visiting for sentimental reasons.

Naji orders a portion of kebab and Hammoudi does the same, too tired to read the menu. Naji takes a quick look around and then tells his brother about that day's demonstration in the city centre. The statue of Bassel al-Assad was pulled down at the very moment when the sun set behind it, bathed in gold. It was a statue of Bassel riding a horse, a poignantly bad rendering. Many hands shook it at the same time, many voices calling out vile curses. When the gigantic horse's rump hit the ground there was no holding back the euphoria. The security forces fled the scene, not having anticipated so many demonstrators. There were tens of thousands of them.

Hammoudi smiles at Naji.

Naji gushes, 'We even burned the Baath Party flag. It felt really good. From now on, that square bears the name of freedom.'

'We should drink to that!'

'They don't serve alcohol here any more.'

'Since when?'

'A while ago now.'

Hammoudi's phone vibrates. Reading the message, he turns pale.

'What's the matter?' Naji asks.

Hammoudi shakes his head and then holds his phone out to Naji. He reads that one of the nurses was caught carrying medicines at an inner-city checkpoint and was shot dead on the spot.

Naji's grey eyes darken. 'We're not an army, we're normal people! Are we to let them slaughter us like lambs?' he exclaims.

Hammoudi cradles his head in his hands. His brother is right, what else can he say? He remembers the young woman's face precisely; her laugh and her confidence in him. Hammoudi feels responsible for her death.

Naji lowers his voice. 'In other towns, people are forming their own army.'

'That'll only lead to civil war.'

'Why civil war? We're fighting against the regime, not against the people.'

This city's always been violent, Hammoudi thinks, and studies his brother's face as though it were living proof of that thought. He sips at his Coke. 'It's not right,' he says.

Naji laughs out loud; Hammoudi feels like a little boy.

By the next morning, Naji has gone underground. Along with other volunteers and defected soldiers, he forms the first brigade of the Free Syrian Army in Deir ez-Zor. At this point, the Free Syrian Army resembles a vigilante group, made up of old men well into retirement and a few enthusiastic younger people. They can't really be referred to as an army at all. They're unprofessional and disorganized. They have no weapons, no uniforms, no vehicles, no safe haven to retreat to, but they know their neighbourhoods like the backs of their hands – and the younger ones gradually learn the art of war the hard way.

Hammoudi hears nothing from his brother for weeks. He worries about him, but his work in the field hospital rarely allows him time to dwell on it.

They come during the night. Amal hears them breaking down the front door of the building but she thinks it's part of her dream and turns over to go back to sleep. The next instant, she's wide awake. She shakes Youssef, sleeping peacefully beside her, and makes him climb down into a small crawl space beneath the floor, a former storage space. The entrance is concealed beneath a rug. Youssef is now on the regime's death list for smuggling medicines, at least according to Luna, who says she heard it from her father.

During the minute it takes the men to get up the building's narrow staircase, Amal pictures everything she might lose: her flat, money, jewellery, her teeth, her dignity, her freedom, her life. She decides not to think or feel at all any more. She's not sad. She's not afraid. She's not angry. There are no feelings inside her now. The stairs creak. They're wearing masks, there are six of them and they have torches with them. The beams cast their light across the floor, then over her bed and finally her body. Only now does Amal notice the power has been cut off.

One of them presses a hand to Amal's mouth and she smells the stench of his nicotine fingers. In the meantime, the others are searching her flat: two of them trash her living room, another the upstairs bedroom and two others, men like butchers, tackle the kitchen. They are deliberately noisy, stuffing her computer, her phone, scripts and anything handwritten into blue plastic sacks. They throw books on the floor, smash porcelain, rummage through the cupboards, slit upholstery and paintings. They do at least allow her to get up and get dressed while they work.

'Are you hungry? Would you like something to eat?' Amal asks the intruder who appears to be in charge. She looks into his red-rimmed eyes with their spaced-out expression and smells that the man is totally drunk. He leaves a trail of alcohol in his wake like a child pulling along a toy car on a string.

He raises his right hand in approval and Amal makes him a Persian omelette with fresh herbs that grow in her kitchen and plenty of laxatives, which she keeps in the top drawer. She fries it in butter and turns it with her bare hands.

The secret servicemen stay for four hours, during which they eat and drink everything they find in Amal's kitchen. Half an hour in, they stop looking for revolutionaries and start gathering up all electrical appliances, any porcelain they haven't yet broken, valuables, and then divide the spoils between them. The minute one of them finds an item he likes, he calls out the name of the relative it will now belong to: 'For Muhammed', 'For little Ali', 'For Marwan', 'For my darling Fatima', or 'For Hibba, so she'll sleep with me again at last'. Their faces are alight. One of them slips Amal's pearl necklace into his pocket, and Amal feels naked and vulnerable. They've made themselves so much at home by now that they've taken off their masks.

As they're preparing to leave, a particularly ugly secret-service man stops in his tracks and walks over to Amal. He grabs her by her right elbow, drags her to the middle of the kitchen and then shoves her away. She lands on the floor, falling on her wrist, which now throbs with pain and starts to swell.

'Have we ever arrested you?' he asks loudly enough for his colleagues to hear.

'No.'

'Louder, I can't hear you!'

'No,' Amal repeats more loudly.

'Have we arrested your father, your mother, your brother?'

'No.'

'So why are you asking for freedom? Do you even know what it is?'

'No,' says Amal, adding a quiet 'not yet'. Bile gathers in her mouth.

Then he orders: 'You have an appointment tomorrow morning. Be there at nine.' There's no need to tell her where.

Before they leave, they scrawl a huge piece of graffiti on the wall of her living room in wobbly, uncertain letters: *Bashar is our god*.

Amal waits for the white Opel to disappear from sight and then goes upstairs, where she finds Youssef rolled up, crying. She strokes his head, though she feels nothing for him at that moment.

'Come on, I'll make you some tea,' she says, removing her hand from his head.

Youssef follows her downstairs to the kitchen. They don't tidy up but they do sit together for hours, telling each other intimate details, whispering and laughing side by side. Both of them sit with their knees drawn up and their heads resting on their hands. Next to them is a bottle of cognac that went undiscovered by the secret service. Sometimes a passer-by's voice reaches them. They take turns to drink; the bottle is a large one.

At some point Youssef puts his hands on Amal's cheeks. She reacts, touching her lips to his, and they start kissing. Amal unbuttons Youssef's shirt, lies down on him. Youssef undoes Amal's jeans and kisses her neck, her collarbones, her ears.

An hour later, Amal leaves the house. It's early morning and the sky is fading from dark blue to white. Rose-tinted light falls on Amal's bare legs. She forgot to put on tights in the rush. The air stands still, as if even it is waiting. Bashar al-Assad smiles benevolently from a giant poster. This week's slogan under his picture is '*Kullna ma'ak*' – 'We are with you', in which the 'we' refers to the Syrian people and 'you' to the all-powerful ruler. Amal has clear memories of the day when Hafez al-Assad died. The radio and even the minibuses broadcast hours of Quran readings, all shops and bars were hurriedly closed and everyone made a show of shedding crocodile tears. People cried and made quite sure everyone saw them crying; and everyone automatically registered those whose eyes remained dry.

Amal called her father earlier to ask for help. Now he's parked his car outside her house, and he takes her things and puts them carefully in the boot. He doesn't tell her off. Even when they get to his summerhouse in Saydnaya, a town high in the mountains with a largely Christian population, he says nothing about either the revolution or Amal's involvement in the demonstrations, for which she is grateful. He stays the night, helps her to light the fire and settle in, then drives back to Damascus the next day. He's going to try and bribe someone at the secret service to cross Amal's name off the wanted list.

Amal spends several weeks in Saydnaya. She likes her father's house, the extravagant architecture, the spacious rooms with rugs, crystal and fireplaces, bright white Egyptian-cotton bed linen, stone bathrooms, the jacuzzi by the panoramic window spanning an entire wall, the underfloor heating. It's no coincidence that Bassel built his house here, of course. The place is known not only for its fresh air, but also for the excellent network of smugglers selling archaeological artefacts from here to the whole world. Even in Bashar al-Assad's palace there's an entire bathroom decorated with artefacts from Palmyra.

Amal is alone most of the time. She walks the austere, narrow streets, always accompanied by a cool breeze, a Greek Orthodox convent rising above the town like a vast despot. Sometimes she climbs the many steep stairs to the convent and looks out at the mountains towering above it. She sleeps badly, tossing and turning for hours before she nods off exhausted as dawn approaches.

She ignores Youssef's messages. He doesn't prove particularly stubborn, though. Their last night together triggered something bad in both of them. Amal feels abandoned by him, and he's ashamed of not having protected Amal from the secret service, of cowering in his hiding place instead of standing by her.

As Ramadan comes ever closer and Bassel assures her the wanted list has been dealt with, Amal returns to Damascus.

Hammoudi's shift starts at five in the morning. He's afraid of being followed so he takes several detours on his way to an unassuming building in a busy area. This is the temporary hospital where they're treating the injured at the moment. It's set up so that it can be moved to another apartment in the space of an hour, if necessary. If they do get found out, though, it's questionable whether they'd ever get away in time.

The stress and the lack of sleep affect Hammoudi more than he'd expected. He can't shake the feeling that something has gone terribly wrong in his life, especially when he follows the lives of his Paris friends on social media.

Hammoudi enters the two-room apartment and says good morning to its owner, a young human-rights lawyer who's already awake and smoking a cigarette. 'I'll let you work in peace,' the lawyer says, although he's still in his pyjamas.

The blinds are closed and the spacious living room is divided by three large sheets. Minor injuries are treated in the front section, while behind the sheets is the improvised intensive-care unit, where patients rarely survive. Having changed into a suit, the apartment's owner brings a pot of strong coffee and says goodbye for the day. He looks just as tired as Hammoudi.

The first patient isn't admitted until noon. He has so many injuries that Hammoudi doesn't know where to start. The nurse too stares in horror at the wounded body, tears running down her cheeks. For two hours Hammoudi tries to save the young man, but it's pointless.

Ten minutes after the boy's death, his mother turns up at the makeshift hospital. She's petite and fragile, her slim face framed by a dark scarf. When she sees her son's wretched body she says nothing. She freezes, even her breathing seeming to stop. Gently, she takes her son's hand. Only now does Hammoudi recognize her; she's his neighbour, Mohammed's mother.

She says, 'I'm glad you were with him. He always admired you.'

Over the past few months, Hammoudi has built an insurmountable wall around himself, but now it collapses with one blow. He has to lean against the wall, his forehead and his palms are sweating, his heart racing. Hammoudi is still staring at the dead boy, whom he can't reconcile with his neighbour. He feels the blood flooding his temples and then feels nothing more as the room around him descends into darkness.

Late that afternoon, Mohammed Mullah Issa is carried through the streets of Deir ez-Zor in an open coffin. Mohammed was top of his class with an extraordinary talent for science, outstanding even for the Bashar al-Assad High School for Gifted Pupils. Hammoudi remembers Mohammed telling him his dreams only a few months ago. He wanted to study and travel the world, building unusual, elegant and strong bridges. He only lived to the age of fifteen.

His mother, his aunt, his sister and Hammoudi's mother wail and whimper. No one can understand their words. No one wants to understand them. Their faces are contorted. Mohammed's father walks alongside the coffin, sobbing, around him a sea of outraged neighbours, fellow students, locals and friends.

Once Hammoudi came round in the clinic, he was told what had happened that morning. The regime ordered the students at all Deir ez-Zor schools to take part in a demonstration in support of Bashar al-Assad. The students reacted with griping and grumbling. They were handed government flags and Assad portraits. The portraits depicted a middle-aged man with cold eyes and a moustache slightly wider than Hitler's. Their procession gradually began to move, the girls dressed demurely in pale grey and pink uniforms, the boys in pale grey and blue, most of them wearing autumn jackets.

Apparently, Mohammed started chanting revolutionary slogans at some point. Hammoudi doesn't know how such an otherwise shy boy suddenly decided to set out his demands, first in a low voice and then, noticing that a few were following his lead, more loudly and confidently. He called for freedom, probably feeling free for the first time himself; and that freedom was the most enticing rebellion he'd ever experienced. The mood in the procession shifted, becoming more relaxed and happier. The boys competed to look as brave as possible in front of the girls, but the girls took no notice of their performance; they were loud enough themselves. Their demonstration had nothing to do with Islam, only with the right of young people not to give in.

At the next crossroads, secret-service men blocked Mohammed's path. They instantly began beating him, first in the stomach, then in the face. The boy was kicked in the chest, the head and the back. As he lay on the ground, barely breathing, the secret-service agent Ayhma Alhamad – the son of the infamous Syrian army general Jameh Jameh – approached him. Ayhma Alhamad was less than two metres away from Mohammed when he drew his weapon and fired the first shot.

It's the first day of Ramadan and it's so hot on the streets that even the asphalt is melting. Everyone is hiding inside, watching TV series made especially for the holidays and taking naps to help cope with their fasting. Many restaurants are closed. The temperature had settled at forty-seven degrees. On the balconies and at the windows, strings of lights are waiting to illuminate the city in the evening.

Today is the premiere of the telenovela in which Amal plays the lead. The producer has invited all the cast and crew to break their fast in a luxury hotel. Only half of the three hundred invited guests have turned up.

The entrance hall of the Four Seasons is decorated with cut flowers and smiling receptionists. Music is already echoing in from the terrace. Although the dress code is informal, the women are wearing long evening dresses, high heels and what looks like their entire family jewellery collection. Amal is greeted with kisses on both cheeks; everyone wants to take a selfie with her and congratulate her. The entire setting appears surreal to her. Yet she too is wearing a long white robe and can barely walk in her matching high heels, and she smiles as though her feet were her only problem in life.

No one present has seen the first episode; it aired late in the afternoon when most people were just waking up from their naps and the housewives were beginning to prepare the evening meal.

Amal joins a group of women exchanging the latest rumours. They talk about who's still in the country and who's going to leave, and when. Out of the corner of her eye, she registers who has had what cosmetic surgery done since she last saw them. A lot of the women have a look of grim determination on their faces. The men, in contrast, are merely freshly showered, if that.

The sun sets and the muezzins' calls sound outside. Fruity cocktails and champagne are served. The guests sit down at the huge, festively decorated table to break the fast together; a fast that no one present observes. From a distance they hear isolated explosions – shooting from the Damascus suburbs. Amal's temples throb. Everyone is at pains not to mention politics. Anyone could be an informer.

The director, a chubby control freak with a firm command of all the virtues of his profession, makes a toast to Amal. He praises her to high heaven and everyone applauds. Amal feels flattered and a little proud. He says that all Arabs feel drawn to drama and that Amal could become the new figurehead of pan-Arab post-drama, and at that moment not only Amal but even the waiters realize he is ridiculing her.

Then he invites Amal to dance, intending to create a Disney-like finishing touch. They twirl briefly around the dance floor before Amal heads back to one of the tables. The director looks amused. They sit down.

'Don't be angry, it was just a joke.' Amal withstands his gaze and refuses to smile; she knows he's afraid of women who don't smile.

He waves a waiter over, takes two champagne flutes from his tray, and once the waiter is out of earshot he says, 'I admit it might not have been the best joke ever.' The music gets louder. He slips his hand between her knees.

Amal remains motionless for a moment. Then she stands up, smooths her skirt and says, 'If you touch me again I'll chop your hand off.'

Amal knows it's time to leave Damascus and yet day after day she delays her departure. She clings to petty excuses, first wanting to wait until it cools down a bit, then until winter's really here, then until her little brother has finished his exams, and then it's almost Christmas and Amal is still in town. People begin to recognize her on the street more and more, only she doesn't know whether that's a good or a bad thing. Above all, she doesn't want to leave because it's the only place where the real version of herself exists – a version in which she has no financial worries for the next ten years, lives in the flat her father bought in her name, and has plenty of jewellery, designer clothes and money in her bank account. What's much more important, though, is that it's the place where she can work in her profession, where her friends and family are, a place where she speaks the language, knows the secrets and customs and where she'd like to start a family of her own.

To be on the safe side, she decides to apply for Russian citizenship, which she's entitled to through her mother. The staff officer at the embassy treats her to a variety of sullen looks but is veritably friendly for a Russian. Seated in front of a huge photo of Putin in a heavy gold frame, he explains she'll need a transcription from her father's family register, which she'll have to apply for at the registry office.

The next day, Amal enters the shabby registry-office building. The corridors are grey, sparsely lit by bare bulbs, and the paint is flaking even from the frames of the Hafez al-Assad portraits. The toilets emanate a foul stench; Amal pulls her scarf up over her nose.

The registrar hands Amal the document through the gap below a pane of glass that hasn't been cleaned for years. The paper is old and yellowed and at first she thinks it must be a mistake – in the 'children' column, instead of just the two names Amal and Ali are three more: Ziad, Ali Nidal and Batool. Their dates of birth coincide with Bassel and Svetlana's marriage; in fact, they're all in the period when Bassel was studying in Moscow and courting Svetlana. But Amal has no time to work it all out; she feels nausea beginning to rise and she runs to the toilet to vomit. She retches and chokes, the entire contents of her stomach flowing into the toilet bowl; a few splashes land on the seat and some behind the bowl, then Amal brings up only bile, and finally her retches are dry. Once she's capable of standing she wipes first her mouth and then the toilet seat with a tissue, her motions hectic. She leaves the cubicle and is grateful that there is no one else in the toilets.

She runs cold water over the backs of her hands and wets her face. She's as pale as death, her hair is tangled and she can't rinse the taste of vomit out of her mouth. She stands there with her arms trembling, exhausted and sweaty, unable to process what's going on. She goes back to the registrar, lurching like a drunk, and asks whether the paper is real. The man glares at her and asks what exactly her problem is, and just as Amal opens her mouth to reply she understands that her father has been lying to her all her life.

Amal drives to Qudsaya along Rabwah Road, past high hills and a snaking stream. She turns into a steep, side street and parks outside an inconspicuous house, its walls unplastered and the upstairs windows secured with metal bars. She hates this neighbourhood because it's so close to the shabiha headquarters. This is where her father's other family lives. She got their address from the registry office.

For an hour, nothing much happens, except that at some point a young woman appears and gets into the car in front, adjusts the rear-view mirror to reapply her lipstick, starts the engine, pulls out and drives off. Amal stays where she is.

Eventually a short, tubby woman in a bright pink headscarf and large sunglasses comes out of the house. The headscarf confuses Amal; it clashes with the image she's had of her father all her life. It was her father who explained to her that the Quran says nothing about headscarves, but that women – especially actresses – should take pains to dress modestly.

She sees the woman hail a taxi and puts her foot down without thinking. Fifteen minutes later, the taxi stops outside an Islamic fashion boutique, its window displaying long-sleeved dresses dripping with rhinestones. The woman gets out of the car, rummages in her handbag and unlocks the shop with a huge bunch of keys as she greets the staff waiting outside, three pale girls wearing headscarves in three different shades of grey.

Amal drives on, leaves her car in a guarded car park, buys chewing gum and Coke at a kiosk and walks back to the shop. It's open now and one of the young women is mopping the floor. Amal enters the shop. Playing the absent-minded shopper, she looks around, her hand running along the clothes hangers. Despite the bright, glittery fabrics, the place feels constricting. Amal's shoes leave dark prints on the freshly washed floor.

'Can I help you?' the salesgirl asks with a shy hint of a smile.

'I'm looking for something for a wedding,' Amal lies, a barely repressible lust for provocation rearing its head.

'How nice! Who's getting married?'

'My father's taking a second wife,' answers Amal.

The salesgirl looks amazed, then embarrassed, and a certain coolness settles between them. She turns to Bassel's wife number two for help as she leaves the storeroom. Amal examines her openly. She looks to be in her late fifties, with a full face and dark eyes framed by crow's feet. Her body is voluptuous and maternal. Amal wouldn't be surprised if the woman smelled of milk. She looks at several dresses but doesn't try any of them on, although the salesgirl encourages her to do so. Her motions are mechanical, she comments on fabrics and cuts without paying attention to the dresses, and then she leaves the shop hurriedly.

Apart from her and a rather drunk man sitting at the bar, the place is empty. Amal orders a beer; the man nods over at her. The bar is dark, cigarette ends and scraps of paper littering the floor.

Amal wonders how often her father must have visited his other family and whether his second family's habits are very different from his first. And which of the families does he count as his first and which as his second?

'I've just found out my father has another family,' Amal says.

'These things happen,' says the man at the bar. He doesn't seem the slightest bit surprised. Amal looks at him closely; he's tattooed all over his body, has a large nose that has probably been broken several times and long, straight hair neatly combed back and fastened in a bunch.

'I was in prison because they thought I listened to heavy metal.'

'You have repulsive taste in music.'

'Will you buy me a drink?'

'Alright,' says Amal, and gestures to the barwoman to bring them two beers.

'Not beer, whisky,' says Amal's drinking buddy.

'Alright, but the next round's on you.' Amal nods at the barwoman, who immediately opens a bottle of Jack Daniels and slowly pours two full glasses. She has a pierced eyebrow and her hair is dyed green. The heavy-metal dude necks his glass and slams it on the bar. Amal sniffs at her glass and then does the same, making sure not to pull a face.

'What exactly did they accuse you of?'

'Devil worship.'

Later that day, as evening approaches, Amal drives back to Bassel's other family's house, slightly drunk. She parks so that she has a good view of the front door and turns off the engine. There's a light burning on the first floor and Amal sees the clothes-shop owner's head dashing around the kitchen. The streetlamps come on and solitary moths circle in their beams of light.

A good quarter of an hour later, a young man walks down the road and opens the front door. He is of average build and average height; Amal can't see any more than that. She shivers in her car.

A little while later, Bassel shows up. A woman walks alongside him, also in a hijab, and Amal assumes she's his secret daughter. But as the front door closes behind them, Amal realizes it's her who's the secret daughter. She can't stand it any longer and gets out of her car, slamming the door behind her. Her legs are trembling. She wishes she could run to Bassel but she can't, not yet. She doesn't have the strength.

Amal has always been Bassel's favourite, the beloved daughter who could do no wrong. She's always got everything she wanted and she was never surprised by that privilege. Now she feels robbed of it for the first time. She's simmering with rage, unbounded disappointment and most of all shame. She's ashamed of her own naïvety, of her father's lies, his devout wife and his illegitimate-legitimate children with their stupid names, children she'll never meet, and she's ashamed she really believed she was worth loving.

The bell's ring is piercing; she hears fast footsteps and then the door opens and the shop-owner is facing Amal. She eyes her in amazement. Eventually she says, 'What do you want here?'

'I want to talk to my father.'

'And what do you think you'll get out of that?' Bassel's wife's face has taken on an amused and arrogant expression. Her question floors Amal; she doesn't know what she wants.

'Let me in,' Amal says.

'No, you've got your own house,' the woman says calmly, trying to close the door.

'Tell him to come out, then.' Amal's voice is exaggeratedly loud and articulated.

'He won't do that.' And she's right. Instead, a lanky boy comes to the door, no older than eighteen, and asks his mother, 'Who's this? What does she want?'

'Ask your father. Ask your father about Svetlana. Get him to explain it all to you. Ask him about Svetlana!' Amal yells. The boy stares at her in horror. He probably thinks I'm some kind of Russian mistress, Amal thinks as the iron door is slammed in her face.

With her lips pursed and her fists clenched, she stands her ground outside the door. She doesn't know what to do next; she waits for the door to open again but it doesn't. After a while, she turns around and returns to her car, shoulders raised and head hanging.

PART II

In the kitchen, Amal takes a last glance at her script and another at the mirror before leaving the flat. The door to the terrace is open. It's probably occupied by snipers again. Amal doesn't check but still locks the front door and the door to the terrace.

Only now does she remember the curtains she was supposed to pick up from the tailor, and goes back. She puts the receipt saying she's paid half the sum in advance in her pocket and runs down the stairs, each of which is a different height. The solid wooden door on the first floor is ajar; the architect has probably just popped out of his office to fetch breakfast.

Amal says hello to the optician whose shop is on the ground floor. He has a thick monobrow and a friendly face, although the lenses of his glasses make his eyes seem supernaturally large. The optician beckons Amal into his shop, which smells of cleaning fluids, and offers her a tea that seems to have a hint of soap to it. Then he says that the satellite dish Amal shares with him – he paid for it and Amal let him put it on her terrace – isn't working. Could he send someone to repair it? Amal doesn't mind.

The sky is pale and cloudless, rain recently fallen. The pavements shine with water, drips glint in the sunlight on the trees' leaves and twigs. The jasmine bushes exude their beguiling scent.

Amal pulls her coat tighter and turns left. She notices there are no cars on the main road – the square outside the parliament is probably blocked off again because Assad's people are holding their demonstration of goodwill outside the building. They're the most passionate supporters, veritable believers holding up photos of Bashar al-Assad – but also of his father and his older brother, who was to have ruled in his place until he was killed in an accident – like icons at an Orthodox service. Among them, though, there are also schoolchildren, students and civil servants, who are bussed to the demonstrations by the government and can't say no.

Damascus is in the grip of the secret police now more than ever. The city's strategic points are under surveillance; the government wants to keep an eye on every demonstration and every gathering. And yet despite all that, Damascus is the place where Amal was born and grew up, the city where she knows the streets and alleys like nowhere else; where she's lived the language and the customs and understands the people, some days more than others. She doesn't want to leave and yet she knows she has no other choice. Perhaps she won't have to stay away for long; that's what she hopes. The new curtains are a testimony to that.

Her heels clatter on the cobbles. The street's many restaurants are crowded already, the smell of food on the air. She turns into the tailor's shop. The owner, a rotund man, gives Amal a discount and hands her a sweet, and she laughs roundly. A plump woman in a black robe enters the shop and starts a flirtatious conversation with the tailor. Amal takes the opportunity to say a quick goodbye.

She strolls past the popular Abu Shaker smoothie bar, a tiny place with photos of the owner, his family and his grandfather – a champion bodybuilder – in the window. The atmosphere is tense. Worry and fear are inscribed on the faces of the passersby. There are a lot of new people in the city, escaping from the fighting in Idlib, Deir ez-Zor, Homs and Aleppo to the relative safety of the capital. Their faces look even more embittered than the Damascans', what with the cares and woes they've brought with them. They match the new sound of the city: the sirens of police cars and ambulances.

Amal passes the parliament building and the generals' club, reaches the Al-Hamra Theatre and looks at the posters for the new productions. The Al-Sham Cinema is closed; officially for renovation but in reality it's for a different reason. The Assad regime is waging jihad on the performing arts and has closed almost all theatres and cinemas. They're building thousands of new mosques instead.

Amal turns right. Outside the Dar al Saalam School, the school of peace, a checkpoint has been set up overnight. The block consists of two cars and five armed soldiers, stopping random people, with impenetrable looks on their faces. They're teenagers, carrying weapons for the first time in their lives and experiencing power over life and death. That makes them arrogant and stupid. Amal smiles at one of the soldiers; he gives an embarrassed grin. To be on the safe side, she decides not to pass the checkpoint. Many soldiers have begun emphasizing their Alawi accent to make it clear they're loyal to the regime. They're everywhere. With their Opels and SUVs, they've even changed the smell of Damascus.

At a kiosk frequented almost only by the secret service, Amal buys a pack of Gitanes Blondes and three flashlights, because there are constant power cuts and she's afraid of breaking a bone falling over in the stairwell.

Amal is hungry but she can't decide whether to get ice cream from Patisserie Damer or just falafel. It's still a little cool for ice cream, so she opts for falafel at the stall next door. She eats as she walks. Over the past few weeks she's noticed she's been followed by a slim boy with a remarkable resemblance to Bassel. Now she thinks she sees him hiding cautiously beyond the next corner. He's probably from the shabiha, thinks Amal, and casts a hesitant glance in his direction. He doesn't look like a government man at all, but perhaps that's what makes him good at his job, she thinks. He's still there, trying to pretend he's looking at a window display.

Amal crosses the road. On the traffic island, the policeman she's seen every morning for years smiles at her and asks where her car is. Amal replies that she's sold it; too many checkpoints, not enough parking spaces and petrol's too expensive. She takes a taxi now when she needs to. She checks for the boy again but he's gone.

Amal goes into Café Pages, where her friend Raajai is sitting with crossed legs in the far corner, flicking through a newspaper. Two buttons of the collar on his snow-white shirt are undone. Raajai studies classical music and plays the harp, which prompts many young men to make false assumptions about his character. Amal puts the curtains in their plastic bag on the table, greets her friend with kisses on each cheek, and sits down.

'How are you?' Amal asks, looking at the dense crown of his eyelashes. She feels a strange tenderness for him, something she can't explain to herself. Maybe I'm in love with him, she thinks.

'Fine,' he says with a smile.

Amal passes him her keys. 'I won't be home till this evening.'

'Thanks,' says Raajai as he pockets the keys. He uses Amal's flat now and then to meet his boyfriend undisturbed. They've been together six months but Raajai frequently complains the relationship is barely progressing.

'Watch out for yourselves!' says Amal, and the two of them stop talking as the waiter approaches. They order two coffees and Raajai laughs out loud while the waiter leaves them. He's an Iraqi; he's known these precautionary measures since the days of Saddam Hussein.

'Are you okay?' Raajai asks, lowering his voice.

'Someone's following me.'

Raajai raises an eyebrow and shakes his head of dense curls. His face is a picture of deep concern, which Amal immediately wants to wave away. She shrugs and says as nonchalantly as possible, 'He doesn't look dangerous.'

'Maybe he's a fan,' says Raajai, and Amal laughs.

As she says goodbye she takes his hand and tells him, 'I'll see you later. You two have a good afternoon.'

'Look out for yourself,' says Raajai. His tone is serious.

'There's nothing I can do anyway.'

Amal crosses a tiny square in the shape of a star and then the Al-Assad Bridge. She looks over at the Flower of Massar, a gigantic construction project on the riverbank, spearheaded by the First Lady. Next to her, a woman is pushing a sleepy child in a buggy and Amal tries to catch a glimpse of the baby, but it's so tightly swaddled she can only make out a dummy between two rosy cheeks. On her right are the former presidential palace and a five-star hotel. Then come the new generals' club and the secret-service headquarters, exactly opposite Amal's institute. A concrete wall is being put up around the headquarters; protection from terrorists is the official explanation from the great leader, whose face Amal has seen about a hundred times on her short walk. Walls are being erected around all the city's secret-service buildings and military facilities, roads changed so much that not even the taxi drivers know their way around Damascus. The regime is preparing for a siege.

Amal heads into the institute through the opera entrance and the secret-service men let her pass; they know her face by now. The nervousness only leaves her once she's safely inside.

When she leaves the building after a strenuous afternoon
of conflicts with her Russian professor, the man who's been
following her for two days is back again. He is pressed against
a wall, smoking. His face is pale and tired. He looks more like
a peeping tom than a secret agent, Amal thinks, and she walks
up to him. As he catches sight of her, his face reflects several
kinds of panic. She takes up position next to him.

'What do you want from me?' she asks, her voice calm.

He stares at her mutely and his gaze harbours longing and
loneliness. Amal dislikes him immediately.

'I'm Nidal,' he says. His voice trembles.

'So?' says Amal.

He looks at her, uncertain.

'What do you want, Nidal? Tell me!' Amal decides to act as
aggressive as possible to get rid of him more quickly.

'Nothing,' says Nidal with a shrug. The light in his eyes is
extinguished. Now he looks at the pavement and says, 'Would
you have a coffee with me?'

Amal nods and at the same time fears she's fallen into a trap.
But something about his posture makes her feel slightly more
warmly towards him, even though he's far from having won
her over.

In the café, Amal immediately lights a cigarette. 'I've seen
you before,' she says, slightly less hostile now. His face is not
attractive but not ugly either. The unpleasantness is probably down to how average he looks – his eyes and skin are
pale brown, almost the same shade, and his hair is boring and
straight as it covers his forehead.

'You're my sister,' Nidal says.

Amal puts her elbow on the table and corrects him.
'Half-sister.'

They hold the silence as long as their nerves permit.

'What was he like to you?' Amal asks in the end.

'Who?'

'Our father.' Amal tries to sound ironic, but fails.

'Strict.'

Amal is visibly surprised.

'A narrow-minded, conservative arsehole who loves no one but himself. Domineering and moody,' Nidal continues.

'Bassel?'

'Yes, your Bassel.'

The waiter comes over. Amal orders a coffee and a glass of water. Nidal orders nothing.

He speaks as if in a dream, still not looking at Amal and seeming to expect no reaction from her either. 'I was a *soft* child for him. My sister and my older brother are normal and nice. Maybe that's why he loves them so much. They don't want any more out of life than to get married, doesn't matter who to, as long as it's soon. My mother is jaded and withdrawn. She hates her husband, she won't let him sleep in her bed and yet she plays the virtuous wife in front of the neighbours and her own children. She makes me so angry! She doesn't believe in God and yet she still covers her hair, she loves gossiping over tea and pastries but she acts devout and self-righteous, and there's a poster of Bashar al-Assad in our house even though she hates politics.'

'Sounds like a perfect family,' says Amal, not without satisfaction.

She's annoyed with Nidal's dogmatic speech, and most of all she's angry that he's burst into her life like this.

'What happened after I left?' she asks.

'Nothing.'

'What do you mean?'

'He went on exactly the same as before. Didn't say a word about it, no sign of remorse, no insight and certainly no regret. He didn't even admit to knowing you, actually. He refused to answer my questions so I thought I'd come and look for you.

Maybe get to know you. My mother must have known every-thing for years; she wasn't at all surprised by you turning up.'

'How did you find me?'

'It wasn't hard. I went to the registry office and they gave me your addresses. If you can do it, I can do it.'

A long, uncomfortable silence follows. Amal stirs her coffee and looks out of the window. Then Nidal leans across the table. 'I went out to your house. To your villa. You know, I had no idea Bassel was rich.'

'Seems like all of us were being kept in the dark one way or another.'

'I don't understand why his entire fortune has gone to his illegitimate family.' He speaks in a tone that demands agree-ment. Suddenly he pauses. 'I'm sorry, but it's just not fair. Your side has a villa and apartments in the city centre, while I'm condemned to living with my mother and doing military service.' Nidal's voice rises.

'He's sending you to the military?' asks Amal, putting her arm on the table. Nidal reaches for her wrist but Amal pulls her hand out of his grip.

'As I said, I guess he was much more liberal with his secret family. I've had a lot of trouble with him.'

Amal feels steadily more uncomfortable. 'I've got to go. All the best, Nidal.'

'Will I see you soon?'

'I don't think so.' She stands awkwardly, drops her bag, picks it up again and dashes out.

Amal is waiting for her father in an elegant, black lace dress in the restaurant above the luxurious Hotel al-Sham. She had written him a long email and asked to meet, and he'd sent a long and warm reply – without mentioning his other family.

Amal's lips are painted red and her face is powdered white. The restaurant itself is not far from her apartment, and most importantly it's expensive. It rotates above the building, commanding an overwhelming view of the city at war. You can even see the explosions on the edge of town. The décor is nondescript, the waiters wear livery and gelled-back hair despite the circumstances, the male guests are in dark suits while the ladies flaunt daring necklines or bare shoulders.

Bassel is late.

Amal orders red wine and plays through the various scenarios in her mind. He'll apologize. He'll say it was a misunderstanding. She'll shout and scream and perhaps lash out. She wonders why her father has lived his life this way – is he a pathological liar or simply a bad person? Might he have had other reasons Amal doesn't yet know? The waiter tops up her glass as night settles over Damascus.

Amal imagines the conditions under which she might forgive her father. She tries to summon her favourite childhood memories, the way her father sang Umm Kulthum songs in the kitchen, very quietly so that no one would notice he was singing. She remembers Bassel taking her to school when he wasn't on one of his extended work trips and gently neatening up her military uniform, which all schoolchildren had to wear at the time.

Bassel doesn't come.

The regime troops approach the city an hour before sunrise. Nidal is on the back seat of the military jeep, his rifle upright between his trembling knees. He has pulled his helmet low over his face. The driver drums his fingers nervously on the steering wheel. The other two check their Brownings again.

Nidal's unit has been transferred to Deir ez-Zor in the east of Syria, close to the Iraqi border. In Damascus they were told they'd be fighting terrorists but it looks very different on the ground; the order is not to attack bearded men and to concentrate solely on the Free Syrian Army. Several of Nidal's comrades have already defected but Nidal can't make the break. He doesn't want to join the Free Army. He doesn't want to join the Islamists. He doesn't want to fight at all but he has no choice.

The tanks forge ahead and destroy everything that gets in their way: traffic signs and streetlamps, shops and houses, statues, schools and libraries, even the street surface. The army approaches the city from three directions simultaneously and blocks off the streets. Nidal watches the thin orange strip on the horizon.

Then the killing begins. The regime snipers spread across the roofs and shoot at everything, even cats. People try to run from death in their slippers. In a matter of minutes, the streets are strewn with wounded and dead. Some utter desperate screams of 'God is great'. What a lie, Nidal thinks. He looks into the faces of the frightened people and is afraid himself.

His unit is radioed commands to get out of the vehicle and assemble with the others at the entrance to the city centre. The jeep stops, the soldiers jump out and line up against a wall, standing to attention. Then they march at the double from house to house, kicking down doors, ransacking homes and taking the men prisoner. They drag them out onto the street, line them up and shoot them. The snipers cover them. Nidal is scared of being killed and scared of killing. He can no longer trust his own senses; he tries to block everything out.

Facing a mother and her two daughters in a squalid living room, Nidal's commander – a tall man with a face pock-marked by acne scars – changes his strategy spontaneously. The mother weeps and wails and says her sons have long since left for Lebanon and her husband, may God bless his soul, died a decade ago. The commander drags one of the daughters away from her mother, shoves her into the bedroom and throws her on the bed. He calls the mother a whore and pushes her against the wall. Then he orders the soldier next to Nidal to rape the girl. She's not even fourteen, so thin that Nidal thinks he might see through her. The soldier too looks like a frightened child. He's only a few years older than the girl. Now he turns his head slowly to his superior and his face betrays perhaps even more horror than the girl's grey eyes. He says nothing, merely shaking his head. The commander, equally silent, aims his gun at the boy's head and pulls the trigger. The girl screams. Blood splashes onto her dress. The commander nods at Nidal now, sweat running down his neck to his back. He doesn't know whether he's ready to die. He doesn't know what he's going to do or what he's capable of. At that moment, the commander receives radio orders to pull back his unit. For the first time in half an hour, Nidal dares to take a proper breath. As he leaves the room he doesn't turn back to his comrade's body. He hears the echo of the girl's sobs for a long time.

By the time Hammoudi leaves the field hospital shortly before sunrise, the smell of decay is already spreading across the city. The dead are lying on the streets, their bodies beneath makeshift shrouds of sheets. Most of them were killed by single shots to the head. The sheets are brightly coloured, blue, red, yellow-patterned – coated in the thinnest layer of sand and stiff with dried blood. Flies whirr through the air; they're larger than usual, Hammoudi notes, as though they'd eaten their fill. Deir ez-Zor has become a ghost town. Some 40,000 people have fled since the previous day, in buses, cars and trains.

Hammoudi's parents' living room is packed full of bags. They can't decide what to take with them so his mother and youngest sister are running around the house, stuffing clothes into cases, unpacking them again, throwing photo albums, books, shoes and medicines into plastic bags before they realize they might need towels and bed linen as well. Hammoudi wipes the sweat from his brow – the fans on the ceiling are at a standstill.

Hammoudi's father, a gaunt man with thick, white hair, raises his voice; it's obvious he's not used to doing so. He says they have to leave in ten minutes, tells the women to put the bags by the front door and he'll load them into the car, and not to forget water.

Once the ten minutes are over they are all actually outside. Hammoudi's mother wraps a thin, white shawl around her shoulders and embraces her son.

'Come with us,' she says and strokes his cheek tenderly. Hammoudi shakes his head and inhales her scent, wishing he could break it down to its chemical components so he could call it up later whenever he wanted.

'You're just as stupid as your brother,' says his mother with a sigh. 'God punished me with two mules instead of sons.'

'Come on, it'll be over in a few months and then we'll dance on Assad's grave,' his father says, with an unconvincing show of confidence.

Hammoudi can hardly resist the temptation to get in his parents' car and simply leave everything behind him, but he's the only doctor left in the besieged part of the city. So he helps his father load up the car and says goodbye to his family. His little sister clings to him. Her whole body trembles. As he kisses his mother's cheeks he can taste her salty tears.

There's so much Hammoudi would like to say to her but he says nothing. If he allowed himself to speak the only thing that would cross his dry lips would probably be 'Take me with you'. Only now does he notice how much his parents have aged in recent years, his mother's face haggard, his father's back crooked, their eyes embedded in dark shadows. They look tired and frightened and Hammoudi doesn't know whether that's the work of the past few weeks or the years he spent in Paris. There, he always remembered them as cheerful and alert; two people who had been happy together for decades.

'We have to go,' Hammoudi's father says and sighs.

'How will you get through?'

'We've bribed the soldiers at the roadblock,' his mother answers, her voice cracking.

'Can you trust them?'

'Naji took care of it all but he won't be able to come to us,' says Hammoudi's sister. She puts on a headscarf; it's the first time Hammoudi has seen her like that. It makes him sad, but it will mean it's easier for her to get away.

'Look after Naji,' Hammoudi's mother tells him. 'I don't think what he's doing is a good thing.'

'At least he's doing something,' says Hammoudi's father.

'That's exactly the problem! He's joined up with some idiots and now he wants to fight!' Hammoudi's mother fires back.

'What other option do we have?' Hammoudi's father asks, but his voice sounds questioning rather than assured.

Hammoudi stays out of the argument; he doesn't understand how it has come to this in only a few weeks – his family refugees, his brother an insurgent and he holding out in a makeshift hospital and operating without pause.

The last word of farewell has been spoken. His parents' car turns the corner and Hammoudi sets off back to the hospital, walking slowly at first. When a bullet hits the ground before his feet and whips up a cloud of dust, he remembers the snipers and runs and runs as fast as he can across the open junction. An elderly woman shouts at him from her window to be careful. He feels infinitely lonely. He wonders whether Claire is still on her own.

Amal's brother comes early in the morning to say goodbye. He's in a better mood than he has been for a long time. The sky too is cloudless and blue, oblivious. Ali has brought her a little gift, which he enjoys presenting. A tiny box that she doesn't open.

'It's a necklace, not necessarily beautiful but it's heavy and it's gold, so you can sell it whenever you feel like,' Ali says, and Amal thanks him and is surprised that her departure seems realer to him than to her.

'Where's your luggage?'

Amal points at two wheeled cases, a black travel bag and a plastic carrier bag filled to the brim.

Ali helps her to carry everything downstairs and stow it in the boot of the taxi. Their goodbye is tense, especially as Ali's face is so blithe and bright. Amal hugs him and tells him to look after himself and to come and visit her. Ali assures her he'll come soon, and then the two of them stand silently facing each other, not knowing what to do next.

It's hot outside, the air flickering. The taxi, an old 1970s Mercedes, has a squeak. The faded leather seats are torn, yellow foam spilling out of them. The driver, stocky with an impressive dark moustache, has agreed to take Amal to Beirut for a hundred dollars. They don't say a word to each other on the way. The roads are narrow, winding and bare. Their sides are strewn with plastic bags and empty chocolate- and crisp packets, blown about by the wind. Amal is still thinking of Ali's carefree face.

The radio plays Fairuz's songs, again; for the first time, Amal can't stand the sound of her voice. She's about to ask the driver to turn off the radio when he brakes abruptly. There's a military convoy ahead of them. Trucks, tanks and rocket launchers are crawling along the road. Soldiers' heads stick out of the sides of the trucks. They have earnest faces, none of them smiling. Tons of steel that will soon be deployed against human bodies.

The driver switches off the radio of his own accord. Amal puts on her sunglasses so he doesn't see her tears. They're not allowed to overtake the convoy so they drive behind it for an hour until they reach the turn-off for Zabadani.

At some point, a text pops up on Amal's phone: Welcome to Lebanon. She has heard nothing more from her father.

The end of September sees in the loveliest season in Deir ez-Zor. Temperatures fall to a bearable twenty-nine degrees and a gentle wind blows through the streets. Children have gone back to school, mothers can finally relax after the long summer holidays, and fathers plan the last family trip out to the desert for hunting and barbecues. These weeks are the most peaceful time of the year – usually.

Nidal's unit has been relocated, now tasked with guarding the Deir ez-Zor military airport, and there's nothing in the world Nidal cares less about than that airport. He spends most of his time alone writing letters to his half-sister; not emails but real letters, written on yellowish Syrian paper of inferior quality. He writes that their father is an arsehole and his mother a tyrant and he's sorry he only met Amal so recently. But perhaps they can get to know each other now. They're long, beautiful letters, which he keeps underneath his mattress and doesn't send.

Nidal's unit moves out again in the morning. They follow a long convoy of tanks. Nidal sits in an open jeep that races along the streets of Deir ez-Zor, hoping he'll never have to get out. He doesn't know what exactly he's supposed to do. His palms are so wet with sweat they can barely grip his rifle. Nidal tries to look only straight ahead so as not to see any dead bodies but they're everywhere, maltreated corpses of all ages, dotted with gaping holes. Their eyes, those that still have eyes, are empty and wide open.

The soldiers herd the people together outside their houses like livestock. The men are immediately picked out and lined up. Then they are shot before the panicked eyes of their wives, daughters, sisters, aunts, girlfriends and grandmothers. Blood pools on the road.

Suddenly, the vehicle in front of them explodes. Steel flies through the air and crashes to the ground. Nidal feels as though all his teeth are being pulled at once. He hears and sees nothing more. Dust everywhere.

He gets out of the jeep with the others. He stumbles, falls down and intuitively closes his eyes. Until he realizes abruptly that he's making a fatal mistake. So he opens them again and presses himself against a wall with all his weight. He runs off and after only five metres he ducks and stands still and runs on as soon as the soldier ahead of him does so. Shots fall, several bullets landing right next to his boots. Nidal receives radio orders to shoot, so he raises his gun, which is miraculously still in his hand, and shoots. He sees his comrade's chest getting hit by several bullets and watches the man collapsing to the dusty asphalt. Not thinking, Nidal crawls underneath the fallen man. Warmth escapes the dying body. After a while, once the shooting has stopped, Nidal gets up. He's alone on the street. Out of his senses, he runs to the next house, the door is locked, he runs on, and at some point he finds himself outside a storage space. He smashes the window with a stone and climbs in.

It takes a while for Nidal's eyes to grow accustomed to the darkness. The stagnant air and damp walls feel like paradise on earth. He moves between the crates to the furthest corner of the room and crouches down, his head leaning against the wall. He's dizzy. Several hours pass without change. The whole room is full of fat buzzing fruit flies. It's muggy and the food rotting away in the heat gives off a foul stench. Nidal thinks he can also smell blood. Intense pain hammers at his temples. He hides behind a few crates, rolls up and waits. In the distance, he hears shots and bursts of dogs barking.

Not until the evening of the next day does Nidal dare to climb out. The street is abandoned, the streetlamps destroyed, and the power has been cut off. A little light comes from the moon shining through the narrow window onto the crates, and from the twinkling stars. Nidal leaves the top half of his uniform in the basement and moves through the city in a vest and camouflage trousers. He left his gun behind because he'd run out of ammunition. Every muscle in his body is aching. His mouth is dry as a bone and his stomach is cramping with hunger.

Walking is difficult so he supports himself against walls as he moves quickly along the streets. He wants to get out of the city, only he doesn't know what direction to take. He dreams of fields and a babbling brook where he could lie down to sleep on the banks.

Something pushes him backwards. He staggers and a burst of pain runs through his left shoulder and then his right leg, his knees collapse, he sinks to the ground. All he feels is someone leaning over him.

Beirut is an ugly and violent city corroded by civil war, capitalism and corruption. On holiday as a child, Amal saw her first dead body here – dangling from a streetlamp above a main road, and no one took any notice of it.

Amal hates Beirut. She hates the gigantic SUVs cruising the streets like tanks; she hates the soldiers' arrogant faces and the way their fingers seem to be melded to the triggers of their machine guns; she hates the modern tower blocks and the wasteland drowning in rubbish between them; she hates the deep holes in the roads, the Hezbollah, the rude taxi drivers and cultural functionaries. She stays with friends for the first two weeks but switches apartments several times, as they keep filling up with newly arrived relatives and acquaintances from Damascus, Raqqa or Aleppo.

Syrian children beg on the streets. Fortune is not on their side, they're thin as rakes, their clothes ragged and their dusty feet in cheap, plastic sandals. Only a year ago, these children were at school and had a future ahead of them. Now they listen to their parents dreaming of returning home. Or moving to Europe. Everyone can recite the prices for smugglers by heart. But only a few manage to get away.

Not until she gets to Beirut does Amal understand she will never lead the life she dreamed up for herself. The life she spent so much time and effort preparing for. She hasn't yet found an alternative to Beirut; sometimes she thinks she'd be better off in Cairo or Istanbul but she doesn't know anyone there and she's scared of being lonely.

She throws her energy into the nightlife. Supressing her feelings has always been her most effective tactic.

During her second week in Beirut, Amal goes to a small bar in the city centre. The music is loud and obtrusive and Amal is long since drunk. She talks to a guy she knows called Sami. He tells her he owns a restaurant and it's doing very well. He's looking for kitchen staff. Amal says nothing, just smiles and hopes she never has to take a job as a kitchen porter, but then she spots Raajai. Sami gets up and says a sudden goodbye. He asks Amal to give him her number and she types it hurriedly into his phone before she embraces Raajai.

'I didn't know you were here!' she exclaims.

'I only just got here today. But I can see you're doing just fine here.'

'Something like that,' says Amal.

'How's things in Damascus?'

'Not much different to here,' says Raajai, and points at Sami's phone, left behind on their table as if by accident. 'I bet it's recording,' he says.

Amal nods.

They leave the bar and walk along the emptying streets. Amal links arms with Raajai.

'What on earth do we do now?' she asks.

'I don't know. Nothing, I guess.'

'Are you planning to stay here?'

'If I find a flat I'll stay, if not I'll go back to Damascus. I don't want to stay and I don't want to go back. Have you got a flat?'

'A room.'

'Can I stay with you?'

'In my bed?'

'Are you single right now?'

'Yes.'

'Then in your bed. Where's Luna, by the way?'

'In Damascus.'

'And your brother?'

'Him too.'

'Isn't he afraid he'll get drafted?'

'My father's paying.'

'It must be nice to have a rich father.'

Amal doesn't answer. She doesn't tell him she has no contact with Bassel any more and her brother doesn't even pick up the phone when she calls him. That he waits days before calling her back and when he does call at last, he only lets the phone ring once, not picking up when she calls back and only enquiring by text message how she's doing, but not expecting an answer to his question. She's tried to talk to him about their father but Ali blocks every conversation. Amal is angry with him, she's furious because he's left her and betrayed her too, but the worst thing is that she misses him. Yet she knows he's fine, even when he doesn't contact her, because he posts photos of himself and his intact little world every day on Instagram.

Raajai gives her a long look but she avoids his eyes, and then he simply puts his arms around her and holds her tight. They stand in a close embrace for a long time.

The inhabitants of Deir ez-Zor are still being massacred. Many of the corpses left behind on the edges of the streets are already bloated. People are found dead in their beds, kitchens, hallways, basements and front gardens, where they are hurriedly buried. The park becomes a graveyard. No one is buried according to Sunni, Coptic, Circassian or Armenian custom now. Instead, corpses and body parts are interred under cover of darkness. Hammoudi has vague memories of cemeteries in Paris that looked like parks, but a park turned into a cemetery has something monstrous about it, he thinks.

He has been operating without a break for thirty-six hours. The operating room is now in the basement of a former private medical surgery, provisionally adapted to provide basic care for patients. The higher floors are too dangerous because of the aerial bombardments. They've given up treating people in apartments; this cellar is their hospital now.

Hammoudi works with one male and two female nurses, a vet and a former circus performer known to everyone only as Little Man. Hammoudi's brother abducted him from an Egyptian circus two years ago, when it came to Deir ez-Zor for a couple of weeks. Little Man's job was to walk around the ring holding a cardboard sign between acts. He had the saddest face in the world. Hammoudi's brother stared at him all evening, then watched the whole show again the next day and stayed on. When the lights went out, he and his seven best friends kidnapped Little Man. They put their unresisting captive in a car and drove him to the best restaurant in town, where they treated him to kebab and got him drunk on arak. Things went on that way for three more days, after which Little Man decided not to go back to the circus. The director had other ideas about his performer's future, of course. He sent armed men after the 'kidnappers', which wasn't a good move, especially in a town like Deir ez-Zor. Follwing a minor knife fight with no serious injuries, the two sides came to an agreement and Little Man stayed.

The hospital staff are volunteers; at night they all sleep together on the first floor of the building, permanently on call. Exhaustion has taken possession of every fibre of their bodies, the exertion is perpetual, their energy is sapped, their feelings numbed. Whenever a bomb falls, and that happens often, so many patients are brought at once that Hammoudi constantly has to decide which life to try to save first. Always knowing that someone else will die as he does so.

Little Man comes in while Hammoudi is changing his shirt. Hammoudi raises his eyebrows and prepares for the next catastrophe. Little Man says Hammoudi's brother has come to see him, and a moment later Naji is standing in front of him. He's wearing black clothes and a black headband. He looks tired, his cheeks are hollow, his eyes ringed by deep shadows, his skin pale. The brothers embrace briefly by way of hello.

'There's nothing wrong with me, I just wanted to see you,' Naji says with a broad grin.

'It's up to me to say whether there's something wrong with you or not,' Hammoudi replies. Naji laughs but immediately turns serious and says, 'I've brought someone with me.'

Nidal is lying on the back seat of Naji's car. His lips are dry, he's pale and can barely breathe. Hammoudi flashes an unspoken question at Naji but his brother merely shakes his head and says, 'I had no choice, he's just a child.' He pronounces his words like an apology.

'We have to make sure no one catches sight of the uniform,' says Hammoudi, pulling Nidal's trousers off. Then they transfer him carefully onto a stretcher. Nidal is in a serious condition. Hammoudi operates on him and then leaves him under Naji's supervision.

At dawn, Hammoudi comes into the sparsely equipped ward. Naji is still smoking, though he has now moved on to hash without tobacco. He has a lot to forget. He's been away from Deir ez-Zor for the last few weeks, getting hold of weapons for the resistance in Turkey, or at least that's what he led Hammoudi to believe. When the military surrounded the city, Naji headed back with a group of ten fighters. They spent twenty hours crawling through the oil fields. But they managed to remain unnoticed. Once they reached the city they began their assault. They were well organized and fully armed.

According to Naji's tally, he killed at least seven soldiers. He thought of nothing as he killed them, felt neither bad nor good. He killed out of necessity – he knew it was war, man against man, and he didn't intend to die, at least not yet. He refrained from unnecessary cruelty, or at least that's what he tells himself. He killed twice with his gun and twice with his own hands; three men fell victim to hand grenades he detonated. Every dead soldier posed one less threat to him. Dead soldiers meant more civilians would live to see the dawn in Deir ez-Zor. He tells none of this to Hammoudi or anyone else. He'll have to deal with it alone.

'I don't have any painkillers I can give you,' Hammoudi says, looking at his brother's upper body. He has several cuts that are deep but not otherwise cause for concern.

'It's alright, just sew me up.'

Hammoudi cleans the wounds and then he sews them with swift stitches. Naji doesn't even grimace.

'You're getting better and better.'

'I get a lot of practice.'

'We always wondered why you wanted to be a reconstructive surgeon, but now I'm glad you did,' Naji says, and Hammoudi grins.

Then he asks his brother in a whisper, 'What's with the black headband?'

'What else can I do?' Naji hisses. 'We're losing the war, we have too many fronts and not enough weapons. The clans are mobilizing too and I don't want to know what side they'll be on. There's no other way to force Assad to his knees. And at least the al-Nusra Front is well positioned. I'm not interested in their ideology, but I do want to fight the regime. It didn't go badly at all for us today. We could win this war.'

'I thought we were staging a revolution, not inciting war,' says Hammoudi.

'Let's get rid of the regime first, and then we can see whether it's a revolution or a war.'

'Hand in hand with the Islamists? What the hell's that going to achieve?'

'Why not? Do you see any other option? We're not ready for a world without ideology yet, and the fighters need some kind of common denominator, no matter how small. Everyone can agree on Islam, so why not?' Naji takes a deep toke on his joint.

Hammoudi shakes his head. He remembers watching hours of footage of the fighting in Iraq with his brother as a teenager, and documentaries about al-Qaida, Saddam Hussein and the Russian–Chechnyan wars, the two of them sharing joints and talking about anything and everything.

Then Hammoudi says to his brother, 'You're taking money

from the Gulf states!' There's no ignoring the despair in his voice.

'And from Turkey. Do you think weapons come for free? Or your painkillers? The Free Syrian Army is going to join al-Nusra soon too.'

Naji notices that Hammoudi's temples are beginning to grey.

Nidal dies at dawn, alone; no one will ever know his name. His letters to Amal are lost too. They're still under his mattress at the Deir ez-Zor barracks.

Amal's craving for success has been extinguished. A year ago, she thought a normal job and an average life would never be enough for her. What she wanted was to be seen, to live another life every night on stage, to make her dreams come true.

She's now found a shared flat in Beirut for about a thousand dollars a month between them – with ancient wiring and no running water. Two rooms plus kitchen and bathroom, a small balcony, plaster crumbling off the walls, water stains on the ceiling and piles of rubbish bags in the building's entrance.

The house is opposite a hospital that is only now being rebuilt. The construction work starts at six every morning with a loud drill concerto. Amal shares the place with two flatmates she knows vaguely from Damascus, girls she doesn't like much, but the three of them manage to scrape the rent together and keep the apartment relatively clean.

Next door to them lives a loyal Hezbollah supporter. He celebrates every new Assad speech with a round of shots from his rifle, shaking the whole house. He keeps a home training machine and dozens of weights on his balcony, from which neon-coloured energy-bar wrappers often flutter down. The local children love catching them.

Everyday life in Beirut is unbearable; people are getting more and more despairing, aggressive and devious. The cost of living is now higher than in London or Zurich and Amal is nearing the end of her savings.

She hasn't managed to find any work so she calls Sami two weeks on and asks him whether the job is still going in his restaurant. He remembers her instantly and tells her she can start straight away; the other girl apparently quit just yesterday.

The restaurant is decorated with mosaic tiles and lanterns, multi-coloured tea lights, tacky mirrors and sequinned cushions, making it look like an Oriental grotto. The kitchen, on the other hand, doesn't even have windows. Amal feels like a coalminer in there.

Sami has four waitresses working for him, all tall and slim, plus a kitchen boy and a chef. Amal's job is to assist him. The chef is in his late fifties, with tired eyes and a large nose. His body is stocky, as though shrunk through hard work. He always keeps a bottle of arak by his side, which empties over the course of the evening. The chef is a taciturn man but still extremely irrational and frightening, so everyone works silently in his presence. When he does feel like talking he yells at one of the waitresses or fires them spontaneously – although he has no authority to do so. The owner puts up with his behaviour because the guests love his food.

On the first evening, the chef asks Amal where she's from. She doesn't reply and his eyes turn hard and derisive. He stands there broad-legged, far from sober.

'I can tell anyway,' he says, followed by an hour of ostentatious silence, his chest tautened. Amal sees a fist-sized tattoo on his biceps, a souvenir of his political convictions in the Lebanese civil war.

Later that evening, as he debones lamb shanks, sliding his knife along thigh bones, he says, 'Your lot occupied our country for twenty years and now you're coming back. You can't imagine what we went through here in the civil war. We had to queue for hours for bread, there was no electricity to be had. And corpses, all the corpses in the streets. They destroyed the whole city. What you're going through is nothing compared to our suffering.'

One horror story follows another, Amal not saying a word. She knows these stories would never be told if she weren't there, but she also knows there's no point comparing suffering. For two days, she feels like quitting and she envisages stabbing the chef in the belly with his knife or at least spitting in his face, but she knows she wouldn't find a new job anytime soon, not as a Syrian. Five days later, Sami takes on two Syrian kitchen boys, one thirteen and the other ten. Amal cries when she leaves the restaurant that evening. The boys almost collapsed under the burden of work and no one could help them. She doesn't know whether she's crying for the boys or for herself.

Winter announces itself by its scent, and Luna comes to Beirut for a weekend visit. She's cheerful, mentioning neither the revolution nor the depressed mood in Damascus. For Amal, her visit is a welcome distraction.

The two of them get into a shabby car with a red licence plate, a private vehicle that functions as a taxi. The driver starts by taking a slight diversion, then he claims not to know the Christian street with its many bars, until he does remember where it is in the end. He drives particularly slowly past the Hezbollah headquarters. Now and then he speaks into his phone in a subservient tone. 'Yes, I've got a girl, a real jewel. But I want two hundred dollars more, she's still a virgin. Yes, mmh, yes, two hundred. She's between fourteen and sixteen. A virgin, definitely.' He eyes them in the mirror and Luna instinctively pulls her skirt down over her knees.

When the taxi stops for them to get out, the driver suddenly demands three times the price. At Luna's amazed enquiry, he merely replies, 'Because you're in our neighbourhood,' and clicks his tongue ambiguously.

'Whose neighbourhood?' Luna asks.

He turns around to the two women and hisses, 'Hezbollah.'

'This area still belongs to the Sunnis,' Amal yells, throwing a small note at him and getting out.

They continue on foot. None of the passers-by look them in the eye, apart from a group of Russian-speaking sex workers who stalk past them on high heels.

Luna has brought enough gossip along from Damascus to lighten the mood again. Amal gets recognized in a bar and a group of young men insist on taking selfies with her. They move on but leave the next bar after minutes as well because the Syrian secret service is sitting there in plain clothes, eavesdropping on the guests and filming them on their phones.

'The bar owner is renowned for giving Hezbollah and the Syrian regime valuable tips – or at least the secret service doesn't have to pay in his bar,' Luna whispers.

'How do you know that?' asks Amal.

Luna shrugs but Amal looks closely at her friend, mistrusting her for the first time in her life. Amal has never asked Luna about her politics. Perhaps she's afraid of the answer.

When the two of them fall drunk into Amal's bed at dawn, Luna says she doesn't understand Amal.

'What don't you understand?' asks Amal, propping herself up on her elbow. She yawns, her eyes burning with tiredness.

'Why you're doing all this to yourself. And to us.' The last words are a murmur.

Amal sits up abruptly.

'It's all just an Israeli conspiracy,' says Luna. Her eyes have an unhealthy shine to them.

'Remember how we had to swear at school every morning to fight the USA, Israel and the Muslim Brothers?' Amal asks back.

Luna nods.

'Why are you starting all that crap again then? We didn't even believe that propaganda at primary school. It was less credible than Santa. And now you want to believe those tall tales, all of a sudden? What world are you living in?'

Luna starts to answer but Amal interrupts her. 'I'm getting a glass of water.' She leaves the bed, warm from their bodies, goes into the kitchen and turns on the tap, which no water comes out of, puts on her shoes and leaves the flat. She walks onto the street, the first people hurrying to work around her and shouting into their phones. Cars, taxis and buses so jammed that they can't drive any faster than walking pace. The air smells of rubbish.

Amal stares at the skeleton of the building opposite, not understanding how Luna could change her position so quickly, how she could change it at all, why she's succumbing now to the myth of an international conspiracy when she refused to believe it as a child.

Amal walks towards the shell of the hospital. She climbs over the fence, walks through the construction rubble and grit. Signs are hung on the ground floor, warning Syrian workers never to leave the premises under any circumstances.

The sun burns down mercilessly on the earth, though it's still far from its zenith. The humidity soaks Amal's dress in sweat. I don't know her, I don't know any of them, Amal thinks. They're like strangers, only even less predictable.

By the time Amal gets home hours later, Luna has left. The bed is made, the curtains are still drawn, and it looks as though she'd never even been there.

Hammoudi wakes at dawn and washes his hands and face. For a while now, he's been thinking about starting praying again, but what good would it do him? Even the suspension bridge collapsed a few days ago. So he shrugs on some clothes and steps out into the hospital corridor. There's a long day ahead of him.

The corridor smells of damp and putrefaction, emanating from the broken corpses. Little Man is sitting on the operating table; Hammoudi shoos him off and he lumbers to his feet.

He knows most of his patients personally. They're neighbours and friends trapped in Deir ez-Zor by the siege. There is neither food nor clean drinking water in the city, never mind medicines. Everything has to be smuggled in, usually along the river, its current no less dangerous than the snipers on the roofs. Diseases long thought overcome have made a return – polio, typhus and cholera. Hammoudi can't do anything to treat them. He sees children dying of common colds. Everyone has a cough, himself included. And everyone is exasperated – by the ruined buildings, the diseases, the bombs, by the cold and hunger. Most people are merely waiting for death now.

Little Man rushes back in and announces that Hammoudi's parents' house has been hit by a barrel bomb. Barrel bombs are water tanks, refuse containers or oil drums filled with dynamite and metal shards or other explosive material. Hammoudi knew it was only a matter of time before the house would be destroyed or occupied, so his reaction is calm. There are no patients to be treated right now; he decides to go and look at the remains.

'Just half an hour,' he says.

Little Man shakes his head but lets him go.

The early morning light is clear and the cold is a shock to the system. The first thing Hammoudi does is look up; no one has left the house without scanning the sky since the bombing started. A lot of them have developed an intimate knowledge of the planes. They know three MiGs will roar over their heads in the morning, coming back twenty minutes later. When there are suddenly only two of them, the locals joke about the missing pilot's health.

Birds are still circling above the roofs but the sky promises a clear day, perfect for bombing.

The city has now been completely destroyed – the asphalt has disappeared just like the inhabitants. The walls are crumbling, riddled with holes from the constant shooting, many collapsed like cardboard. Some buildings are nothing but skeletons. In others, Hammoudi can make out traces of normal life: children's drawings on the walls, crockery, dried-out potted plants, single shoes and family photos among rubble, waste, glass and bricks. For the first time, he realizes how many tons of brick make up a city. The walls between the houses have been knocked through so the inhabitants don't have to go out on the streets but can move from house to house. On one street, a burnt-out bus provides protection from the snipers' random shots.

Hammoudi remembers the carefree times in Deir ez-Zor, the picnics beneath the fruit trees in the park. He thinks of Rand, the girl he was in love with all the way through school. She had long black hair that tumbled down her back and the

biggest collection of marbles in town. He once wrote her a
note, which his five-year-old neighbour was supposed to give
her, but even though Hammoudi bribed him with cake the boy
simply rang at Rand's front door instead of giving her the letter
secretly. Rand's mother, a very strict woman who watched
over her daughter like a guard dog, immediately informed
Hammoudi's parents and made a point of complaining to the
headmaster about Hammoudi's rampant sex drive. And Rand
paid less attention to him than ever.

Every part of town is blocked off by soldiers. People formed
armed vigilante groups at the beginning of the revolution, to
stop the army from entering their neighbourhoods. Now one
part of the city is under siege by the state army and bombed
every day, and the other part is still under regime control.

Hammoudi is stopped by a fighter. He barks his questions:
who is he and what is he doing here? When Hammoudi
answers, the man suddenly kisses him on the cheeks as
though they're old friends and apologizes, saying they're just
concerned about the locals' safety, Hammoudi has no need to
worry.

'Are there many left?' Hammoudi asks.

'Only four families.' After a brief hesitation, he asks, 'Do you
remember me?'

Hammoudi shakes his head.

'You operated on me a few months ago.'

'And how are you now?' Hammoudi asks.

The man doesn't answer, instead giving a high whistle that
brings a ten-year-old boy ducking out of a ruin. He has a dirty
face and looks too small for his age. The fighter tells the boy to
accompany Hammoudi.

Hammoudi says, 'I was born here, I know my way around.'

The boy grins. 'There are snipers everywhere. You won't get far on your own.'

The two of them set off. They pass ruined houses, burnt-out cars and looted shops. The walls are sprayed with graffiti.

The boy says he's scared of dying alone. He'd rather be with his mother and sisters when it happens. His father died in the early days of the revolution, he says, and now he wants to follow him soon. Just not alone.

They see a man sitting by the rubble of his house, staring into space, and they pass him silently. The sun plays on the roof where a tireless sniper is concealed. There are mattresses and tubs of sand on the street, which the few remaining people use as protection from the shooting. They still get hit. The shutters of the burnt-out and looted shops are down and remains of furniture clog the narrow lanes. The goods the shops once sold are long gone, just like their owners. Only the poorest and most vulnerable have stayed.

Another fighter calls Hammoudi's name and beckons him over. Coming closer, Hammoudi recognizes his cousin underneath the mask. He looks ten years older, though only a year has gone by since they last met. He pats the boy's shoulder and lets Hammoudi continue alone.

Standing among the rubble of his street, the street where he was born and grew up, Hammoudi can no longer tell which house is his family home. He stares at the pile of rubble and shards.

After a while he finds the last remains of the gilt and velvet furniture. One wall, with the expensive wallpaper, the family photographs and the Arabic calligraphies, is still in one piece. He pulls out two rugs that have survived the attack and decides to take them. He throws them over his shoulder and heads back. Two hundred yards on, he puts them down on the ground and goes on without them.

Suddenly he hears helicopters. They circle above his neighbourhood like locusts, flying lower and lower, and soon the side hatches open. A huge cargo is let down. It floats slowly in the sky as if in no rush, and then a gigantic column of black smoke rises from a multi-storey residential building. The sky fills up with dust and darkness. Afterwards the walls lie collapsed, like a house of cards, between the neighbouring buildings. People run in every direction, Hammoudi sees some of them rushing to the bombsite to drag the injured and the dead from the rubble. He too runs to them. At that moment he hears a loud whistle. The whistle is a good sign; it means the grenade isn't meant to hit you personally. Hammoudi breathes a sigh. Suddenly the ground shudders beneath his feet; Hammoudi hears nothing this time. Glass shatters and shards fly through the air. Pieces of wood shoot past him. He's thrown against a wall and strangely enough, his last thought is of Claire. When he comes round everything is dark and quiet. Gravity has got the upper hand again. He smells garlic, old, very old garlic, chlorine and urine. Hammoudi can barely breathe, he feels like dust and rubble have settled inside his lungs. His ears are ringing. His back is nothing but pain.

There's not a cloud in the sky, as is so often the case. It's eleven in the morning, twenty-seven degrees, the air is heavy with exhaust fumes, cars and buses sound their horns, taxi drivers yell, fruit- and tissue sellers cry their wares. The humid air clings to people's bodies like a damp blanket.

Amal spots Youssef at a falafel stall on the opposite side of the road. It's a coincidental encounter and at first she considers simply walking by, but that seems silly so she goes up to him and smiles.

Youssef presents a miserable picture, his hands in his pockets, his head lowered, looking starved in shabby clothes. Luna told Amal he disappeared months ago. She thought the secret service had arrested him. Seeing him in Beirut is akin to a miracle; Amal knows only too well that very few people ever return from the regime's torture chambers. Then again, there is no return after torture – body and spirit are equally broken. Later, Youssef will tell Amal he was arrested for driving through Mezze 86, the Alawi quarter. The security service noted down his car registration and came for him the same day. He was interrogated for three days, mainly on the subject of what he was doing in that part of town. By the time he was due to be released, his file had turned up. Youssef has tried not to remember the rest since then.

Amal greets him with exaggerated friendliness, clearly surprising Youssef with her trusting approach. He gives her a quick, embarrassed look and then fixes his eyes on the ground. Amal's face is radiant and clean, her hair in a neat bun, her fingernails unvarnished and cut short.

'How long have you been in Beirut?' she asks.

'Only a week,' Youssef answers hastily. Even his voice no longer sounds like him.

'Shall we sit down?'

'If you've got time,' says Youssef.

Amal sits down while Youssef stays on his feet. It takes him a very long time to say nothing.

'I've got to go to work in a minute,' she says, instantly overwhelmed by guilt.

Youssef simply shrugs.

'I'd like to see you later,' she says, hesitant. She doesn't quite understand where this sudden desire for Youssef has come from but she doesn't want to let him go.

'Amal, this isn't the time for declarations of love.'

Amal laughs and Youssef watches her brush a strand of black hair behind her ear, and then he asks her at last. 'When do you finish work?'

'I don't know exactly,' she says quietly. 'What are your plans?'

Youssef shrugs again.

'Here, take my key,' she says barely audibly, and when Youssef doesn't react she whispers, 'Please. I don't know exactly when I'll get off work. I work in a kitchen and I don't want to stand you up. My flatmates aren't here, they're visiting their parents in Damascus. I'll write down my address and the code for the door. It's not far. Youssef, please, wait for me there.' As she speaks she takes Youssef's hands. They're both aware this is a gesture Amal learned at the institute. Youssef's hands go limp in Amal's.

It's well after midnight when she gets home that evening. Youssef is sitting in the kitchen – there's a bowl of salad on

the table and a dish of fresh bread. Amal smiles and uncorks
the wine she stole from the restaurant. They eat without
talking much. Amal knocks back two glasses of wine. She'd
like to apologize to Youssef but she can't remember what for.
Frustrated, she pushes her glass away.

'Shall I top you up?' Youssef asks.

'No, don't!'

Amal leads Youssef to the bedroom. The windows are wide
open but the only air coming in is swelteringly hot. Youssef is
embarrassed and stops in the doorway but Amal pulls him after
her. They embrace in semi-darkness. Amal smells of soap and
kitchens.

'Come,' she says.

Youssef raises his eyebrows but she unbuttons his shirt and
gently eases him out of it. The topography of his body speaks
a clear language. It's not only thinner, it's also covered in scars.

Noticing Amal's examination, Youssef looks down at his
thighs in embarrassment. She kisses his neck and asks him
to lie on his front. Her bed sags in the middle; three months
ago it belonged to a stranger. Amal rubs Youssef's back with
oil left over from better days, scented with eucalyptus. She
tries to loosen his muscles, working her way slowly down to
his lower back. There too, he has several wounds that are not
yet healed. Youssef relaxes gradually, closes his eyes and falls
asleep.

As day dawns, they wake closely entangled and stay that
way, not kissing. Pale blue light passes through the broken
blind. Amal strokes Youssef's cheek and her hands are suddenly
everywhere, as if a dam had broken. They look each other in
the eye. Her gaze is slightly absent, his concentrated and full
of desire. He strokes her body feverishly, his fingers feeling for

the thin lace of her knickers, her thighs and belly beginning to tremble at his touch. She grips the headboard and when she comes she throws her head back. Then Amal puts her hands on Youssef's shoulders and sits up matter-of-factly.

Hammoudi is making tea when a young mother comes in with her baby. She's been shot by a sniper, the bullet passing through her shoulder from front to back. The baby wasn't hit, because the mother attempted to shield her with her body – the little girl has only a few scrapes from falling, which Hammoudi examines while a nurse tries to calm her down.

After that comes an elderly woman, also with a gunshot wound; the sniper hit her ribcage. There's nothing more Hammoudi can do for her. She's followed by two boys with kneecaps smashed by bullets and an old man who's had a heart attack. Hammoudi doesn't have time to look at the old man. He operates on the two friends at once, dashing from one table to the other. He manages to remove the bullets but he can't say whether the boys will ever walk again. Hammoudi hopes they'll be smuggled out of the city later. The hospital is not safe and doesn't have enough space, so after major surgery the patients are moved to private homes converted to medical wards.

A young girl has been hit in the belly and chest by several bullets. When she's brought in, still in her summer dress, she's pale, with severe pain at every breath and a torturous cough. Her dark hair is soaked with blood. Hammoudi decides to operate. He sews up her wounds with household needles. His scalpels are blunt. He suspects that only a few ribs are broken, though he has no X-ray equipment to confirm that. The girl holds out on the operating table for half an hour, then dies.

Hammoudi doesn't even have time to take a breath or close the girl's eyes. He rushes to the next patient. A fifteen-year-old boy has a vertical thorax tangential shotgun wound, injuring not only his lung but also his spleen, liver and kidneys. Here too, Hammoudi decides to operate after a brief hesitation. But another bomb has just fallen and the victims are brought in one after another. Some of them have better chances of survival than the boy. Hammoudi treats them first and hears the boy dying in the next room. It feels to Hammoudi as though he'd killed the boy; he might have been able to save him if he'd had more time.

He treats a grandfather and his ten-year-old granddaughter. They both have severe burns and broken bones. The girl's face is turned to stone, her clothing covered in white rubble dust. When the shock wears off, no one manages to calm her down; she screams and lashes out.

A man brings his son's dead body. His daughter is carried by helpers, both legs torn off; the mother and the youngest daughter, a baby, died in the ruins of their home. The man stares into space. He was at the market looking for food when the bomb was dropped. Hammoudi operates on the daughter. She's given artificial respiration by a converted device for asthmatics, one of Hammoudi's innovations. But when there's no clean water, electricity or anaesthetics, even the best improvisation is no use. The girl dies. She didn't live to see her eighth birthday. The father rocks her body in his arms and strokes her cheek. He leaves the hospital with the corpses of his two children.

Afternoon comes around. A helicopter circles above them, undecided as to whether or not to drop its bomb. When Hammoudi used to hear helicopters landing above the hospital during his training in Paris, it meant an organ was being delivered, or a severely injured patient for whom there was still hope. Hope is a stranger here now. But still, Hammoudi has time for a short break and some food. A neighbour has brought him half-cooked potatoes, with profuse apologies – she didn't have enough kerosene to boil them for longer. It's bordering on a miracle that she got hold of anything edible in the first place. People pick dates from the trees, catch fish, cultivate a few vegetables to survive. The only bakery still operating is on the way to the old airport. Their bread is as hard as rock and there's not enough to go around. People are hungry, and hunger is the most effective weapon – because it dehumanizes. Some roam abandoned homes in search of old tinned food. They still feel guilty when they break down locked doors.

Over and over, Hammoudi escapes to his daydreams, imagining living in Paris again and sitting in his kitchen on a cold grey November morning, the leaves wet on the ground and swirled up by the wind. He drinks a café au lait, listens to the radio with a croissant on a plate in front of him and Claire on the other side of the table. She's wearing his T-shirt, which is much too big for her; her nails as ever are bitten to the quick and her tangled hair is down. She's telling a story that makes her laugh.

Then, at the end of the day when the sky is dark, illuminated only by occasional rockets, a pregnant woman comes into the hospital, accompanied by her husband. The child is in the breach position and the mother needs a caesarean section. When Hammoudi holds the tiny girl aloft, the nurses cry. For the first time in months, a moment of joy.

It's Amal's first day off this month and she collects Youssef from his new job at a building site. He's grown stubble and has white paint on his dark curls. A glimpse of his grey hair to come, thinks Amal, and for the first time that thought doesn't scare her but makes her happy. They hug in the semi-darkness. The place smells of new PVC floors, acrid paint, wall filler and sweat.

They walk home together as night falls. Youssef has stayed in Amal's flat without either of them consciously deciding on it – they get on better now that they rarely speak. The days are good, full of care and something like love.

They cross the neighbourhood with its elegant colonial-era villas, balconies cascading with flowers, orange and lemon trees in terracotta pots and private security crews outside high fences.

The further they walk, the more run-down the houses become. There are washing lines on the balconies, faded sheets, bright tea towels and children's clothes drying in the humid air. Syrian accents become more common and people seem agitated, jumpy, some aggressive. Many are still hoping to return to Syria soon.

They're yearning for a world that no longer exists. There are signs on some buildings warning Syrians not to be seen on the streets after dark.

It's dark by the time the two of them reach their own neighbourhood. Amal's hand is safely in Youssef's when a group of young men in dark clothes block their way, clutching machine guns.

'Your papers,' the teenage leader demands as he points his AK-47 at Youssef's face. His tone is a military bark. He has a very loud voice, probably to disguise uncertainty, and he's the smallest in the gang. The others group themselves around him as though he needs protection.

Youssef holds his ID out to him and the teenager studies the name, place of birth and passport photo at length.

'Arms up!'

Another member of the militia pats Youssef down.

'What are you doing here?'

'Taking a walk,' Youssef replies.

'Lie down on the ground,' the leader orders them. 'If you move a muscle my friend will shoot you.'

Amal and Youssef lie down in the dirt as a single streetlamp flickers on. That gives the young man with the AK-47 the idea of shining a flashlight at them both. Then he gives Youssef a kick. Amal shouts out.

'You're not going to occupy our country again,' another boy says, and then he spits on Amal's head while Youssef receives more kicks. The leader stands to one side, his legs wide and his face becoming ever more relaxed. After a few minutes, he signals to his men to stop, pulls a handgun out of his belt, aims at Youssef and shoots a couple of times.

He deliberately misses his target.

An NGO has announced it's sending humanitarian aid. It would be the first delivery in a long time and Hammoudi imagines what it might contain: painkillers, thrombosis medication, saline solution, anaesthetics, syringes, bandaging material, surgical instruments. The delivery has to be collected from the Turkish side of the border; international organizations left Syria some time ago.

In the grey light of dawn, Hammoudi prepares for the journey with a smuggler from the Hamidiya neighbourhood. They pack water, dry flatbreads and petrol into an old ambulance drummed up by one of the nurses, which they hope will help them through the Free Syrian Army's roadblocks. Before they leave, the smuggler presses a rifle into Hammoudi's hands and says, 'For you.'

Hammoudi won't take it. 'You keep it, I'm not going to need it.'

'Oh yes, you will. Here, take it, it's loaded. When I give you the signal you have to shoot.'

The smuggler places two more guns in the driver's cab and turns the key, but the engine won't start. He tries it again; on the third attempt, it finally complies.

'Nice,' Hammoudi comments drily.

'Let's get going,' says the smuggler, pulling out of the parking space and lighting his first cigarette.

A year ago, it took four hours to drive to the Turkish border; now it's at least seven. Hammoudi would never get through on his own – there are countless checkpoints and roadblocks, and not even the smuggler knows them all because they change on a daily basis. At each checkpoint, travellers have to know exactly what to answer. Asked about profession, it's important to be careful – actors, mathematicians, lawyers and doctors, especially gynaecologists, are regarded as enemies of God, at least at the Islamist checkpoints. At the regime checkpoints they're enemies of Bashar, equally divine, and are executed on the spot. At the Islamist roadblocks there are tests of religious knowledge: How often does a Muslim kneel during morning prayer? Officially it's five times, but it can vary – only the ultra-religious know the correct answer. Responses have to come without the slightest hesitation. And accents have to be adapted to the situation too. Even in a region controlled by the regime, the roadblocks can be occupied by all kinds of groups – and then there's no option but to guess which answer is the right one. Syria has become a microcosm of city states.

Other than sand and occasional sagebrush shrubs, there is nothing to see on the road. The windows are closed to keep out the dust, so the inside of the ambulance is soon hot and stuffy. They drive along dirt tracks, the vehicle shuddering as Hammoudi's eyelids get heavier.

An hour later, he is rudely awakened by a loud bang. The ambulance is parked between the ruins of a burnt-out farmyard and the driver is tapping away at his phone like crazy.

'What's up?' Hammoudi asks.

'There's a problem,' the smuggler explains.

They hear artillery fire but neither of them reacts. Their fear reflex has long since dulled. The driver stares at his phone, which keeps signalling new text messages arriving.

'It might be a while,' he says after a long pause.

Hammoudi turns aside and falls back to sleep.

The battle goes on for several hours. The driver smokes his way through a whole pack of cigarettes while he contacts his informants and tries to find a new route. Once the rattle of machine guns grows quieter he starts the engine again. His informants report that some of the troops have defected to the Free Syrian Army, including a general who is now being sought.

After the city of Raqqa, the scenery gets greener: eucalyptus, cypresses, bitter cucumber vines, apple trees and palms appear. Hammoudi is awake again, chewing on a piece of bread.

'Shall I drive?' he asks.

The driver booms with laughter. 'If I let you take the wheel you'd kill us both. And I don't want to think about what they'd do to me if I told them our only doctor was dead.'

As dusk draws in they reach the border crossing, where two Syrian and two Turkish flags fly only thirty metres apart in the bluish light, between them a concrete wall topped with barbed wire and an iron gate with a plastic arch curving over it.

The soldiers on the Turkish side open the gate and wave the ambulance through. Hammoudi and his smuggler breathe a deep sigh of relief. There are no border guards on the Syrian side any more; they've been driven away by the Free Syrian Army.

'The air's totally different here, eh?' says the smuggler as soon as they reach the Turkish country road.

'I miss the snipers,' says Hammoudi.

'It's so quiet here,' the driver says.

Hammoudi stretches his back. It's almost peaceful.

The aid-organization office is on the edge of a small provincial town. When they get there after a twenty-minute drive, the smuggler says goodbye until the next day and Hammoudi takes a small room in a cheap hotel. The building is run down but the room is quiet, with running water for a shower. He turns the taps and undresses slowly in the bathroom. Then he stops, pulls his boxer shorts back on and runs back into the room. There, he grabs his telephone and calls Claire's number. It rings for a long time but she doesn't pick up.

He's put off calling her for so long because he didn't want the connection to break down in the middle of the conversation or an emergency case to come in. He wanted to talk to Claire in peace, even though he knew he wouldn't have anything new to say to her. He wouldn't go back to Paris. But right now he feels like he could leave at last. If she asked him tonight to go back to France, he'd find his way to Istanbul and get to Paris somehow. It would be enough for him if Claire only said she missed him. On that thought, he falls asleep.

She still doesn't pick up the phone the next morning, either. Hammoudi gets ready and asks his way to the NGO building. It's not far but he still gets lost several times on the unremarkable roads of the small town. When he finally arrives, there's a young man outside the gate, selling sesame rings. He looks like an informer, or at least he's far less interested in his work than in scrutinizing Hammoudi.

The reception is small with two fans gently rotating on the ceiling. Hammoudi asks the man behind the counter about the boxes he's supposed to pick up and take to Deir ez-Zor.

The man, a timid administrator with fat thighs, starts a hectic search for Hammoudi's name and the hospital in his files, finding neither. Beads of sweat form on his forehead.

'Can I see your ID?' he asks.

'Of course,' says Hammoudi and hands him his old French doctor's ID card. The man studies it closely.

'One moment,' he says then, and goes into a back room. A few minutes later he comes back, provides no explanation but gives Hammoudi a sheet of paper with which he says he can collect the promised boxes from the warehouse, and adds, 'You have to wait until the warehouse opens.'

'When is that?'

'In a couple of hours.'

'Could I please speak to the director?' Hammoudi asks.

'I'll have to see.' The man buries himself in his files.

'Our situation's really serious. We have no medical supplies or equipment. I don't want to be ungrateful but we urgently need help.'

'The director will be in this afternoon. Try again later.'

'I can't wait for hours, I have to get back straight away.'

'I'm sorry.' His teeth protrude from behind a smile.

Hammoudi waits. He sits down on a plastic chair at the back of the room, closes his eyes and tries to block all images from his subconscious.

The warehouse doesn't open until around noon. The warehouse manager doesn't turn up but the man at reception takes pity on Hammoudi and takes him to the back of the building.

He hands Hammoudi two boxes prominently printed with the United Nations logo. The boxes are neither large nor heavy, to Hammoudi's disappointment.

'Do you know what's in there? What we need most is bandages and medicines, painkillers, anti-thrombosis medication, surgical instruments. Pretty much everything.'

'I don't know. You can wait for the warehouse manager though.'

'Thanks anyway,' says Hammoudi, and takes the boxes outside to where the smuggler is waiting impatiently in the ambulance. He asks him to get in right away so they can get back before dark. They load the boxes and set off.

At some point, a Turkish police car approaches them with sirens wailing. Hammoudi's driver curses the policeman's sister and mother by turn but still pulls over. When the officer knocks at the window, he flashes him a friendly smile and winds the window down.

'Hello,' says the police officer.

'Hello,' reply Hammoudi and the smuggler, in perfect sync.

'Papers?'

Hammoudi hands him his doctor's ID.

'What is this?'

'My doctor's ID card.'

'Have you got a proper one?'

Hammoudi gives the policeman his Syrian passport.

'It's expired.'

'I know.'

The officer shakes his head and then asks the driver, 'And you?'

'I don't have one. Bashar al-Assad never let me have an ID card,' the driver says.

'What are you doing here?'

'We've been collecting humanitarian aid for our hospital in Deir ez-Zor,' Hammoudi says. His voice conveys great concern.

'Can you prove that?'

'I can show you the receipt,' says Hammoudi, and holds it out to the officer.

'Please let us pass, we're doctors, we have to get back. Our patients are waiting,' says the smuggler.

The police officer takes a long look at the papers and then studies their faces before finally handing back the proof and saying with a smile, 'Alright, off you go.'

'Damn,' says Hammoudi once the policeman has withdrawn to his patrol car and driven off.

'I hope this whole trip was worth it,' mutters the driver.

'I'm going to have a look,' says Hammoudi, pats him on the shoulder and walks round to the back of the ambulance, where he opens the boxes at last. The only thing in them is condoms. Hammoudi digs his hands into both boxes in the hope of finding at least a syringe or some paracetamol, but instead there are only different flavours, strawberry, chocolate, banana, the occasional tutti frutti. For the first time in years, Hammoudi is on the brink of tears.

'What have we got?' the smuggler asks.

'We have to go back. They can't do this to us!'

'What's in there?' asks the smuggler, not slowing the ambulance.

'You're not going to believe it,' says Hammoudi as he climbs back into the passenger seat and holds up a pack of condoms.

'Nothing else?' the smuggler asks.

'No.'

'We'll have to ask Naji to take care of it.'

It's quiet in the flat. Amal's flatmates are out. Youssef is curled up on the bed in their room. The curtains are partly drawn.

Amal looks at him. His hair is spread over the entire pillow, his face pale and his lips feeble, half-open. His face is relaxed and looks almost happy. Amal kneels next to the bed and notices the thin coating of sweat on Youssef's upper lip. Suddenly she's scared. She touches his cheek but the skin is cold. When she turns him on his back, his right hand drops lifeless to the floor and his chest is not moving. She feels for his pulse but she's too nervous to find it. She screams at Youssef, over and over, but there's no reaction.

Amal dials the number of an emergency department at a private clinic, shaking Youssef with all her strength. He gives a low moan.

'Youssef, if you die on me I'll kill you. Wake up, you idiot!' she yells, raises his upper body and shakes him again, his head falling to one side. She runs her hands over his face, punches his sternum awkwardly and keeps jolting his unconscious body.

Ten minutes later, she hears ambulance sirens and there's a knock at the door. Youssef's breathing now consists of gasped intakes and his skin has a bluish shimmer to it. Amal opens the door and three paramedics storm into the flat, find the right room and get to work on Youssef. They pull up his eyelids and shine a light at his pupils. Their motions are precise and coordinated.

'What has he taken?' one of the men asks.

'I don't know,' Amal replies.

Youssef's T-shirt is cut open and a stethoscope applied to his chest while the third ambulance man measures his blood pressure, which is very weak.

'See if you can find a packet, any kind of medication,' the paramedic tells Amal.

Amal runs into the bathroom and finds the floor scattered with crumpled towels, cosmetic products, bottles and tubes. The drawer where Amal and her flatmates keep their medicines is untouched and there's nothing in the kitchen either, until Amal looks in the bin – a large empty packet of sleeping tablets. She grabs it and runs back to the ambulance men.

When she gets to the bedroom, Youssef's face is half-covered by a transparent oxygen mask, an infusion inserted at his elbow. The bed is surrounded by open medical cases. One of the paramedics hurriedly shaves Youssef's chest with a disposable razor and then affixes several electrodes to the grazed skin to connect him to the ECG. They all stop moving for an instant. Amal and the men stare at the line of the ECG, now installed at the end of the bed. Amal starts sobbing. But Youssef's condition seems to stabilize, so two ambulance men take the medical equipment downstairs and return with a stretcher. They load Youssef onto it and carry him carefully down the stairs, one step at a time.

In the ambulance, Amal strokes his hair and cries. The paramedic says, 'He'll make it, we'll just have to pump his stomach. If you'd got home ten minutes later, though, he'd be dead by now.'

Youssef is allowed to leave the hospital the next evening.

Amal and Youssef stay together – they cling to each other like an old married couple and their relationship gains a foundation for the first time. They talk about books they read before the revolution, about films, childhood memories, first crushes – giving each other back a veneer of normality. Their sex too is regular and unexcited, which doesn't make it worse. They've found refuge with one another.

In the middle of the night, Hammoudi is abducted from the hospital. Five armed men come into the operating room and order him to go with them.

They at least have the decency to let him finish the operation he's performing. Outside the hospital, they throw a sack over his head and push him into a car.

Not a word is said during the drive. When the car finally stops, Hammoudi is dragged out of it. They're in the desert, near an oil field. Hammoudi can smell it. Now he's ordered to take a few steps; he feels the rifle barrel against his back. They take the sack off his head and he sees several pick-ups and masked fighters.

It's a clear, starry night. Hammoudi could name most of the constellations. Instead, he watches a pale foreigner prepare for a beheading in the headlamps of the pick-ups. A young local man with his hands and feet tied kneels between two men in ski masks. Something about the masked men's body language makes Hammoudi suspect they're not Syrians. Later, he'll find out he was right. But at the moment Hammoudi is still trying to work out what's gone so terribly wrong in his life.

Next to them is a line of boys, also masked, looking up at the older men in awe. One of the higher-ranking jihadists reads a prayer and the executioner lowers his eyes to his own fingers. They are clutching an ordinary kitchen knife with a faded pink grip, but it's extremely sharp and longer than his hand. Hammoudi looks at the boys again but the masks conceal any emotions. The condemned man closes his eyes. Not a word passes his lips. He's accused of being a fighter for the Free Syrian Army.

Hammoudi turns his head away but the man guarding him from behind takes him in a stranglehold and forces him to watch the scene. His fingers claw into Hammoudi's flesh.

The boy's head falls to the ground. The executioner bends down and picks it up, slowly. Someone pulls out a mobile phone to document the man's death. That someone is Abu al-Qaqa Al-Almani, a man who once left Hamburg for Deir ez-Zor and has since become fluent in the language of jihad.

The boy's body remains in the same kneeling position. Hammoudi is shoved back into the car and driven back to Deir ez-Zor. He understands the warning but it barely makes a difference, partly because he still feels obliged to his patients and believes he has no right to leave the city.

The next night, Hammoudi is picked up from the hospital again. This time it's a short drive. His blindfold is only taken off inside a house, and his hands and feet are kept tied. The room he's standing in is spacious, furnished with large silk rugs and expensive cushions.

Hammoudi sees a small, round figure. He has large ears and eyes with bags beneath them, and a downward-pointing nose that looks stuck on. The emir in charge of Deir ez-Zor is enjoying a generous breakfast – cheese, butter, bread, pancakes and a whole carafe of banana milk – greedily wolfing down his food.

Behind him is Hammoudi's old schoolmate Zair, once a philosophy student, then a fighter for the Free Syrian Army, then the al-Nusra Front and finally Daesh. He's neither tall nor short, neither stocky nor thin, and his face too has nothing remarkable about it. His eyes, though, are intelligent and absolutely cold, not revealing a single human impulse. Eyes that harbour infinity. His men obey him blindly, the tiniest motion of his head enough to make them leap to their feet. Hammoudi has operated on him three times in the past two years, but that hasn't necessarily strengthened their relationship.

'Did you enjoy the viewing yesterday?' the emir asks, with unmistakable loathing. His chin is shiny with grease.

Hammoudi says nothing, merely staring at Zair. Zair stands up to his gaze; in fact, his mouth forms a grin that looks inhuman.

While the two of them keep their eyes on one other, the emir gives a pompous and overblown speech using only the simplest and most easily comprehensible words, probably due to his modest education, three years in a mud hut in the Nile delta. Once he's finally finished, Zair says, 'You can go now. We'll call you when we need you. And say hello to your brother from us.'

From now on, Hammoudi is called upon by Daesh men on several occasions as their private doctor; they bring him their fighters and demand that Hammoudi gives them preferential treatment. They don't bring any medications but they do close down the hospital whenever they're present. While Hammoudi treats the injured, three fighters stand behind him at all times, watching his hand movements and keeping the barrels of their guns pointed at his back.

Amal wakes at dawn soaked in sweat and tries to get her bearings in the empty new flat. Youssef is next to her, sleeping peacefully. They're lying on a mattress, without sheets but underneath a duvet. Youssef's arm is dangling from the edge and he's snoring. First he takes a breath with a loud grunt, then he emits it again with an insect-like chirp, with a frighteningly long pause between the two. It's one of the few nights since they arrived in Istanbul that he hasn't had nightmares.

Life became increasingly unbearable in Lebanon. All they thought about was money and how to get it. Amal's wages were far from enough to make ends meet, and after spending a day in hospital for observation Youssef lost his job and his boss refused to pay the wages he owed him.

They couldn't even afford the basics needed for survival any more. Food prices were too high, and buses, doctors and above all the rent were too expensive. They were at their wits' end, so they decided to move on to Turkey and make their way from there to Europe.

Amal gets up and goes to the kitchen for a glass of water. The flat belongs to friends of friends, who have moved out and left nothing but an old bed, two folding chairs and a sink – for a horrendous price. Next to the sink are two glasses, two drying plates, two forks, one large and one small knife. Amal opens the window shutters. The dawn creeps into the room, soft light playing on the kitchen tiles. The wallpaper is curling in several places, with occasional tears. She sees no one out on the street.

Amal and Youssef have run out of money. Amal has even sold Ali's goodbye present. They'll have to spend several months working in Turkey to finance their trip to Europe. Unfortunately, they have nothing to offer the Turkish labour market – they're just another two Syrians with no prospects. Still, Amal is glad to have left Beirut.

Checking in at Beirut Airport, they had excess baggage and the desk agent said they had to pay one hundred and forty dollars. After a dramatic pause, she added that if they'd prefer to pay only one hundred dollars, Youssef should put the money in his passport. The woman accepted the bribe nonchalantly and put it underneath her phone.

Trembling with cold, Amal goes back to bed. Youssef has got up in the meantime and Amal hears him turning on the bathroom tap. He comes into the bedroom with a towel wrapped around his hips and hands her a cup of coffee. He's wearing grey slippers that Amal hates, but she's grateful for the coffee.

Amal and Youssef walk through Gezi Park, the crows in the famous trees now the only other visitors. Here too, there is nothing left of the revolution. Each of them keeps to themselves their impressions of the new city and their worries over what lies ahead. Only their hands, Youssef's right and Amal's left, never let go of each other.

Istanbul too is full of escaped Syrians. They hear Arabic in bakeries and phone shops, Syrian children try to sell roses to the tourists and are shooed away like flies, entire families camp out in underpasses, waiting for nothing.

When they get hungry they go to a kebab shop not far from İstiklal Avenue. The place is simple enough, a giant doner kebab rotating sedately on its spit. Now and then, a thin man slices meat off it with an oversized knife, puts it on flatbread, adds lettuce, tomatoes, onions and lots of sauce, rolls it all up neatly and hands it over the counter. Loud music plays.

Later that day, it pours with rain. People dash along the streets with their heads ducked, the city now looking grey. Passers-by loiter outside shops waiting for the rain to let up and street cats flee to dry spots. Cars slow down, their tyres spraying fountains of water.

Amal and Youssef spend the rest of the day in an internet café where the air is permeated by cold cigarette smoke and flat-beer fumes. They look at photos of ships and boats on Facebook, comparing prices and reports of others' experiences.

'It's like booking a cruise,' Youssef jokes.

'Our first holiday together,' Amal replies.

'Or we could take a plane: Greece to Germany, Austria, Norway, Poland or Belgium, 3,500 euro; Greece to Sweden or the Netherlands, 4,000 euro.'

'Too expensive.'

'Even a passport is 600,' Youssef reads. 'You just can't look like an Arab.'

'Do you think we'd get through?'

'You might. My skin's far too dark for the border checks.'

Amal looks outside; the streets are still wet. She watches drips of water dissolving into puddles.

As they leave the internet café, the sky brightens. The grey cloud cover has disappeared and the puddles glint in the evening sun. Now the atmosphere takes on something light and summery, the street cafés gradually fill up again and the cats come out of their hiding places, and then the streets cool down and grow dark. The cold creeps beneath their jackets and Youssef strokes Amal's wrist, a gentle touch.

The sun goes down. Hammoudi waits for the battle that always begins at sunset. He's alone in the hospital, the last patient taken to a safe house a quarter of an hour ago, directly after a seven-hour operation. Hammoudi performed it by the light of a mobile telephone, under the influence of uppers he gets from a fighter whose leg he once saved.

As he's looking for his phone, he feels a hand on his back.

'Don't say a word,' comes a hoarse whisper in his ear. The voice seems vaguely familiar.

'Naji?' Hammoudi asks.

'Were you expecting someone else?' his brother replies.

They hug and then Naji says, 'Listen, I've only got five minutes and then I have to go. Hammoudi, you have get out of here, tonight.' His voice sounds like someone who's decided to give up.

This isn't good, thinks Hammoudi, and he says, 'I've been hearing that all my life.'

'No, listen, Daesh is coming to the city tomorrow. They killed the emir an hour ago, we have to get out. Zair has issued a fatwa against you. You're a fair target from now on.'

'I operated on that arsehole just two months ago.'

'Exactly, you do your work without rhyme or reason. Zair has sworn loyalty to Daesh and believe me, you're right at the top of his list. He won't show mercy.'

'What's mercy got to do with it? I'm the last living surgeon in this dump,' says Hammoudi.

'Listen, I really haven't got time for this. You have to leave

today. Another dead doctor's no use to the revolution. Here.'
Naji hands Hammoudi a small package.

'What is it?'

'A travel voucher.'

'How are you getting out?'

'We've made a deal, they'll let us withdraw tonight. After
that the city's theirs. I'll say it again: Zair is ambitious. He'll
come for you. You have to leave town.'

'What are you going to do?'

'I'm leaving too. Do you want to come with us?'

Hammoudi shakes his head. Naji embraces him one last
time before he disappears into the dark. In Hammoudi's hand
is an envelope containing several thousand dollars and two
packs of cigarettes. Hammoudi sits down on a bed and lights a
cigarette. He inhales slowly and deeply and thinks about what
to do next. He knows he'll die if he waits until the morning,
but he feels guilty towards his patients.

Suddenly the generator springs back to life. The ceiling
lamp comes back on. Hammoudi looks around. The room
is in chaos: the beds are messy, the sheets are covered in dirt
and blood, the ground is strewn with crumpled, blood-soaked
clothing, the medicine cabinets are empty. Hammoudi hates
this place.

Youssef gets a call from someone he used to know, a Syrian TV producer. They're filming a TV series directly on the Syria–Turkey border – Amal could play a minor part and Youssef could assist the director. They're in a small fish restaurant on the Bosporus when the call comes, eating unspecified white fish caught and frozen in Norway before being defrosted and served in Istanbul. They watch the freight ships heading ponderously for the Black Sea. There are dolphins there too, or at least that's what the waiter tells them. A street dog keeps skulking up to their table and waiting with dignity for leftovers.

Youssef negotiates with the producer on the phone. The shooting will last three weeks and the fee should be enough to cover the crossing to Europe.

Youssef raises his eyebrows at Amal; she nods.

Youssef accepts the offer, whereupon Amal tops up their raki glasses, dilutes the alcohol with water and says, 'It's not like we have a choice. So we'll make another series.'

Five days later, they travel to the south of Turkey where the filming is taking place. The crew has recreated a pre-Islamic town between Kurdish villages. There's a market with stalls selling leather slippers, household goods, fabrics and jewellery. Alongside them, cages hold live chickens. In front of the ruins of an old caravanserai, a former inn for passing caravans, workers have erected a huge blue wall for shooting landscape scenes. The landscape itself will be added in the studio using an image-processing system. There are also several apathetic horses and two camels, desperately trying to evade a crowd of children gone wild. The kids – extras who turn up in front of the camera at the oddest moments – romp around in long robes.

The series is set in the first year of the Islamic calendar. Amal is already in costume – she's playing a dancer – her hair not covered, her breasts squeezed into a tiny bra that jingles with gold coins, as do her hips. It's not real gold.

Amal enjoys being an actor again at last. Doing what she's learned and what she loves makes her feel she's being seen as herself again and not just as service personnel.

Most of the actors sit around in costume, smoking, drinking sweet tea out of paper cups and exchanging rumours like hard currency. Although many of them are Assad supporters, they treat each other with caution and respect, as if politics had nothing to do with them. The production company has booked up half of the second-best hotel in Mardin for them.

Shots sound now and then in the distance. To keep the cicadas quiet, the production assistants fire a gun and try to film in the brief periods of silence that follow.

Amal smokes with a muscle-shirted costume guy. They talk about nothing much, the cold, the food. Colleagues come and go, and at some point Amal is left behind with a former fellow student.

'How long have you been out?' the woman asks.

'About a year.'

'It's better that way.'

'Is it?'

'Of course.' She puts out her cigarette and says, 'I want to get out too, but not for my sake, for my brother's.'

'Is he in the army?' Amal asks.

The costume woman nods.

'What does he do?'

She puts her arm around Amal's shoulder and whispers in her ear, ignoring her question, 'Does Youssef know anyone who could get him to Lebanon? I know he's got connections.'

'I'll ask him tonight,' Amal says.

Amal films all her scenes within a week and decides to spend the rest of the time in Mardin, waiting for Youssef to finish his job. But the filming gets more and more behind schedule.

A huge jet, normally only used for intercontinental flights, takes Amal and Youssef to Izmir. They rent a room in a run-down hostel in the Basmane neighbourhood. The corridors are cramped and dark. The floor, its linoleum recently cleaned, smells strongly of chlorine. Everything here is old, the carpets are worn, the furniture ragged, the plates chipped. Three boys are playing football in the back yard, a toddler riding a tricycle around them.

They don't go to see a single sight. They don't visit any bazaars and they don't stroll along the seafront. They stick only to their neighbourhood, where clothing shops in the side streets by the station sell life vests, many of which look fake, and are. They stock them in different models and in children's sizes and in pink or with pictures of Disney heroes. The cafés and snack bars are full of Syrians and Afghans at all times of day and night, smoking manically as they wait for people-smugglers and miracles. The entire neighbourhood speaks Arabic now and the main commodity traded at the market is Syrian gold jewellery.

By day, Fevzi Paşa Street, leading from the station to the sea, is crowded with people whose faces can no longer be washed clean of hopelessness; bustling up and down with one eye always on the shop windows. But as night falls, the street dogs wake after dozing elsewhere in the sun all day and roam in packs in search of food. Street traders spread their wares on Fevzi Paşa: worn trainers, old jeans, single buttons, stolen smartphones and electrical scrap; the street market of a Third World country.

Amal orders a tea and opens one of the two books she brought with her from Damascus – *The Night in Lisbon* by Erich Maria Remarque and Anna Seghers's *Transit* – only to be joined almost immediately by a gaunt man. He's wearing black jeans, a black sweater and an equally dark sleeveless jacket. He has no backpack or bag with him.

'Where do you want to go?' he asks.

Amal stares uncomprehendingly at him at first and then answers, 'Europe.'

'Of course,' he laughs. 'Who doesn't?' He takes a pack of cigarettes from his pocket and holds it out to Amal. When she shakes her head he lights one for himself. He still hasn't introduced himself, and he smokes slowly. His legs are crossed.

'France would be nice,' says Amal, scrutinizing the man.

'What do you want there? Go to the Netherlands or Sweden. Or Germany, if need be.'

Amal sighs, closes her book and puts it on the table. Then she asks tonelessly, 'How much?'

'I'll give you a good price,' he says, pulling Amal's serviette closer and scribbling a number on it. 'This is for Michael.'

When Amal raises her eyebrows he adds, 'Michael, like Michael Jackson. Give him a call.'

Amal doesn't reach an agreement with Michael, but after several other attempts she finds a smuggler who says he'll take them to a boat in a few days' time. He accompanies them to a jeweller's shop in the centre of Izmir, its windows full of diamonds and gold. The jeweller is a slight man with thick glasses and a suit cut from good, dark blue cloth. With a polite gesture, he opens a door at the back of his shop and asks them all in. Amal, Youssef and their recruiter descend a narrow staircase. The basement room is submerged in a cloud of smoke, the walls plain, the furniture functional. There are money-counting machines on several tables, piles of dollars and euros all over the room. Amal and Youssef aren't the only customers; in front of them in the queue is a bull-necked man and before him a young Iranian couple, neither of them much older than twenty. When Amal and Youssef reach the front of the queue, they hand the agreed sum to a haggard man and get a piece of paper in return, noting the sum of money and the name of their smuggler. The note is ripped in two. As soon as Amal and Youssef arrive safely in Italy, they'll call the jeweller and he'll give the smuggler his fee, minus a small commission. If they get sent back to Turkey they can collect their money from the jeweller.

That evening they go out for a meal together; it might be the last time. Amal is impressed by the restaurant Youssef has chosen. It's very quiet with no music to influence the mood, the mosaic wall beside their table shimmers in the candlelight, the glasses and crockery are thin and the plates large.

Youssef takes out a small square box and places it in the middle of the table. The blue velvet bears the golden emblem of a well-known Syrian jeweller.

Youssef says nothing and Amal starts to feel uncomfortable.

'Aren't you going to say anything?' she asks him.

'Aren't you going to open it?' Youssef replies.

Amal eases the box open. It contains a thin ring of white gold.

'It's my grandmother's ring, the packaging is just camouflage,' Youssef says. 'But what's much more important: will you be my wife?'

Amal nods. Youssef puts the ring on her finger. It fits perfectly. Still, Amal always imagined the scene would be more poetic.

Looking at the ring on her finger, Amal thinks that they might die together, the very next week. An abyss opens up before her and thoughts of all kind come streaming out of it.

'We could always stay here, you know,' she says.

'But what kind of life would that be?'

'I don't know!' Amal shrugs and looks back at her engagement ring. 'Maybe three kids and a dog?'

'The children might not go to school, we wouldn't find work and we'd be dependent on Erdoğan's mercy. We're here illegally, Amal. And apart from that, this country will soon go to the dogs as well. It's already starting.'

Amal drinks a mouthful of wine and asks, 'Does that mean you'd like to have children?'

After the meal, a sense of romantic duty prompts them to take their first walk along the ice-cold promenade, where men with menus under their arms stand outside empty cafés and try to entice guests in. After that they go to bed, nervous, and cling to each other in sleep. They ought to be happy, but they're afraid.

White pick-ups appear at dawn, most of them Toyota Hiluxes; just like the Syrian secret service, Daesh also has a preferred make of car. Black flags fly on their roofs, bearing a message in white: 'There is no god but God, and Mohammed is His prophet.' The leaders of the al-Nusra Front have made a deal with Daesh – they can take the city but without spilling blood. The al-Nusra Front retreats overnight.

By the next sunset, sharia law is introduced and penalties and taxes are imposed. Meetings between men and women not directly related or married to each other are forbidden. Smoking is banned. Music too. Everyone has to observe the prayer times, preferably at the mosque. Anyone who doesn't pray regularly and is caught by the religious police is sent to the front to dig trenches. Many of the worshippers' bodies emit a sour smell, just like the prayer mats. People find themselves in a different universe.

Women disappear from public life. They have to cover their faces and are no longer allowed out without male escorts. From now on they move through life quietly – they are not allowed to speak or laugh loudly. Their bodies are swathed in several layers of dark fabric so that no one can even guess at their shape. The only sound they make is the rustle of their clothing.

Most schools, which were already only teaching sporadically in basements, are closed down. All worldly subjects, including mathematics, physics and biology, are removed from the curriculum and even medical degrees are reduced to three years. Instead, young children are put into Islamist camps. If they do learn sums, then they chant: 'One plus one makes two, God willing.' The plus sign is forbidden for allegedly symbolizing the Christian cross. Restaurants between Raqqa and Deir ez-Zor have to remove all dishes except lamb and rice from their menus. Even juice bars are shown no mercy. A malign peace settles over the streets.

The fighters wear black masks, removing them only to eat or when with their families. Some of them are disillusioned soldiers who have defected to Daesh, others local mercenaries interested only in the pay, and then there are the sadists and fanatics infatuated with an illusion of themselves, the most dangerous of all. They all take Captagon, which makes them even more arrogant and takes away their fear.

The city dwellers gather secretly with their neighbours in whichever house still has a working generator. They charge their phones and exchange the latest news – who's been arrested at which checkpoint, whose daughters have been married off, who's been killed. Their phones replace the outside world.

Since they left Damascus, their life has been nothing but provisional and their belongings have been reduced at every stop along the way. They haven't been able to collect any evidence of a life together. Perhaps they will in Europe, if they make it there, Amal thinks.

Now they're facing the task of squeezing their remaining belongings into a single rucksack. A tatty orange blanket belonging to the hostel is thrown over the double bed, with Youssef's directing diploma on top of it. Amal doesn't have a diploma; she didn't have time to finish her degree. Her make-up is spread out next to the blanket: tubes and pots of creams, mascara, lipsticks, powder, primer, foundation, nail varnish, soft brushes – she'll have to leave it all behind at the hostel. Against her better judgement, she brought her backless black Chanel dress with her from Damascus, a gift from her father, and a pair of soft black velvet court shoes that go with it so wonderfully. Now she has to say a final farewell to them. Perhaps they'll have enough time to sell them.

They conceal documents and money on their persons, wrapped in cling film and taped to their skin. Amal sews her few remaining pieces of jewellery into her bra, especially the rings and earrings – she doesn't want to end up depicted in a European magazine as a floating corpse with her grandmother's ruby studs in her earlobes. Over that a practical T-shirt, a sweater and a thick jacket. At the very top of the bag, they tuck in a few lemons; they're supposed to be good for seasickness.

The smuggler arranges to meet them two days later at the Izmir bus station. He makes them walk around town for three hours, from one crowded square to the next, until they're finally loaded into a black minivan. The van takes them to a flat in the south. The driver is an incredibly fat teenager with bumfluff on his cheeks. He's wearing a Star Wars sweatshirt and he drives like he's trying to get them all killed. Cutting across three lanes on the motorway, he holds a cigarette in his right hand and his phone in the left.

After half an hour they reach their hiding place, in an unappealing high-rise estate on the side of a mountain. The estate actually consists of only three buildings in a row, but they're so gigantic they could house entire villages. Youssef holds tight to Amal's hand and they walk after their glaring driver, past dirty pools of water and a heap of rubbish. A pack of dogs roams the back courtyard in search of leftovers.

They enter a stairwell with no light and then an apartment that's equally dark and ice cold. It has only one room and there's no tap in the toilet. The grey linoleum is coming away from the floor in places, revealing a dark substance that really shouldn't be inside the floor of a residential building.

Two brothers are already waiting in the room, Ziad and Mazen. They want to go to Sweden, to join their oldest brother. Ziad has a stocky body with thickset legs, whereas Mazen is tall and long-limbed. A little later, they're joined by a fifty-year-old woman and her teenage son. She's an English teacher from Aleppo; her son is autistic. Then comes a young woman travelling alone with her baby. The father was murdered before the birth, by a government barrel bomb. Amal studies the baby closely, the bare back of its head, the fuzzy hair, its chubby arms and legs. It's always ready to flash a smile at the world.

Another few hours later, five young men turn up, hoping to escape the military and the militias. They spend the whole time playing on their phones. All of them now wait together in the thirty-square-metre flat, the door locked from the outside.

Nothing happens on the first evening. The teacher performs her prayers, her son watching mutely. One of the boys explains the rules of Candy Crush Saga to Amal. The lights go on in the building opposite but no one dares to switch them on in their flat. One mattress lies next to another, their bodies necessarily touching. The men's snores keep Amal awake. The baby wakes several times too and cries to be breastfed.

Nothing happens on the following day either. People come with water and a little bread, feta and olives, but none of them will say when the group will be leaving – and so the waiting people tell each other stories. They don't exchange memories of their past lives in peacetime; instead they tell anecdotes about other attempts at crossings and vague hopes for the future. The waiting is good practice for death.

The English teacher was on a boat headed for Italy six months ago, and there was a massacre on board. A group of people from Sudan were locked below deck without water, food or sufficient oxygen. On deck were Syrians and Afghans. The travellers on the lower deck revolted, at first against the crew, but when they didn't find them in their hiding places they killed the other passengers. The English teacher from Aleppo and her son were among the few survivors. They were spared, perhaps because of the boy's condition. Or perhaps because they played dead and hid beneath corpses.

The boys have also attempted a crossing before, in a rubber dinghy. At some point they were stopped by a larger ship from Greece, crewed by men in military uniforms and black masks. They pointed weapons at the refugees and took all their money and valuables, then destroyed their boat's engine; they drifted for hours before the Turkish coastguard tugged them back to Turkey. Now they want to try to get directly to Italy. As they tell their stories the sun goes down, submerging the furniture and faces in gentle light.

During the third night, a tall man suddenly turns up in the room and bellows commands in Turkish: 'Let's go! Get ready! COME ON! ARE YOU DEAF OR SOMETHING?'

Once again they squeeze into the minivan, and once again it's the overweight teenager at the wheel. He yells into his phone, his voice hoarse. His words veer wildly to and fro, utterly convincing Amal of his insanity. Then he suddenly stops by the side of the road, cuts the engine, calls someone else and then drives back to the estate.

'What's the matter?' asks the English teacher.

The driver takes his foot off the accelerator and explains to his passengers with a shrug, 'Difficulties with the police.'

The mother fiddles with her headscarf. The mood in the van instantly alters – unbounded disappointment mixes with secret relief at delaying the journey at least a little. Utter silence.

That night, it takes Amal a long time to find a comfortable sleeping position, and she tosses and turns from one side to the other. She wishes she could get up and leave the apartment forever, but the door has been locked again. Not until sunrise does she fall asleep with her arms folded, wrapped in her coat. Youssef lies awake alongside her.

The next day they make it to the beach. The smugglers tell them to wait in an abandoned restaurant. Battered wooden chairs on top of the tables, plaster peeling off the walls and the yellowed summer menu still hanging above the defrosted freezer: milkshakes, sorbet, dairy ice cream, iced coffee, chocolate floats.

More and more people arrive, entire families, most of them with small children. They all crouch on the damp floorboards. The children's teeth chatter, their lips turn blue.

Three hours later, they are divided into groups of a hundred people. The smugglers are armed and yell abrupt orders. Families try to stay together and Amal too clings to Youssef.

Then inflatable dinghies turn up. Although they're only allowed to approach the boats one group at a time, chaos instantly breaks out.

It's difficult to get into the boats because their surface is smooth and wet, and Amal keeps slipping off. The smugglers in the boat make no attempt to help anyone, calmly watching the events with their weapons cocked. Amal throws herself in and then pulls one foot after another in behind her. She's already frozen through and soaking wet. Youssef helps the young widow. He carries the baby above his head, hands it gently to Amal on the boat and looks out for the mother, who can't swim and is afraid of the water. The young deserters help the autistic teenager and his mother. Amal sees that several groups have to stay behind on the beach for lack of space.

The boats start off, riding the waves at a sedate pace, and the coast gradually becomes a slim strip on the horizon; at the same time, everything around them grows quiet, only the stars shine brighter. They steer a course for the open sea.

Half an hour later, they catch sight of the mother ship. It's not the modern freight ship they were promised but an old freighter that looks like it's due for the scrapyard. At least it has a steel hull, which calms Amal's fears slightly.

Boarding takes hours and is no less dangerous than the journey itself. Several passengers fall into the water, only to be pulled out frozen stiff and scared to death. By the time they're all on board they notice there are already many people waiting there – some of them have been there for the past four days. A few have a long journey across the Sahara behind them. The ship smells of old sweat, stale air and damp clothes that have been worn too long. It's now full and ready to make its way to Italy.

The ship's interior is built to transport logs and not people – there's only a single narrow ladder leading to the space where several hundred souls sit tightly packed on the floor. Syrians, Palestinians, Afghans and Iraqis; men and women travelling alone, elderly people and entire families with babes in arms. Bodies crammed together, touching one another, legs knocking into other legs, shoulders leaning on other shoulders. It's the middle classes escaping; the poor remain behind in the refugee camps. It's the people who once hoped for more from life than simply reaching a safe country, who once had ambitions and a future.

Amal is the first to go down, followed by Youssef with the baby, whose name is Amina, and then comes Fatima, Amina's mother. It's cold and noisy, the air humid and stuffy and the floor covered with plastic sheets and occasional rugs. The weight of their wet clothes presses them down, they tremble with cold. They are allocated seating spaces, which they are not to leave at all on the journey because the ship is so overloaded that the freight has to be precisely distributed.

With the ship tossing to and fro on the waves at night, Amal doesn't get a moment's rest. She hears her neighbours' coughs and the retching sounds when someone gets seasick, babies crying, old men praying and the engine humming. It all builds up inside her head, which threatens to explode. The swell is strong. Amal pulls her sweater up over her nose, wanting to protect herself from the warmth of other bodies, their expirations and odours, unwashed and unshaved for days, from the smell of faeces, bile and vomit. The floor is covered in a sticky yellowish substance.

When she wakes her limbs ache. Youssef is asleep and Fatima is playing with Amina, who gurgles with laughter. Amal fights her way to the exit hatch, clambers over sleeping people and climbs up on deck. The sea is calm, the surface glinting in the sunlight. She takes a deep breath and her lungs fill with fresh sea air. For the first time in days, she feels hunger and thirst. A boy dashes over from the wheel, barely older than fourteen, by the look of him. He asks her to go back down below deck – the ship is officially sailing as a freighter under a North Korean flag.

Something like a community comes together on board, tenuous links are formed, people share the few reserves they still have: food, cigarettes and nappies. An Eritrean who's picked up some Arabic along the way talks about the lifelong military service in his country and the despotism of the ruling class. The Syrians tell of barrel bombs and poison gas, until at last the memories of better days suppress all stories: a month of peace, schooldays, the scent of freshly baked bread. Men take out their phones and show off photos of their children holding out in Syria, Egypt or Turkey, waiting to be brought to Europe legally.

Late that afternoon, the ship's floor suddenly springs a leak and water slops onto the carpets and plastic sheets. A skinny boy from the crew comes scrambling down with a welding device.

The engine is turned off and without its own impetus, their freighter can't compensate for the high waves. Several people start vomiting. The cabin boy goes on welding unperturbed.

'This is crazy,' Youssef whispers.

'We're going to die,' Amal notes laconically.

Youssef presses himself to her more firmly, but the cabin boy manages to repair the leak. The passengers applaud him and pat him on the back and the ship soon resumes its course. Amal falls into a deep and dreamless sleep.

Shortly before midnight, the ship stops; the passengers grow restless and call for the captain. A few minutes later he actually turns up – an athletic man in his mid-thirties who would clearly rather be doing any other job in the world than this one. He explains to the anxious crowd that they're waiting for deliveries. The smugglers got their calculations wrong; the ship doesn't have any blankets and not enough drinking water. His voice is firm and authoritative.

The crowd grows displeased. 'You're waiting for more people!' an elderly man calls out.

'No, just for supplies,' the captain claims.

'We'll all go down if we take on any more people,' says a young woman. A murmur of agreement passes through the crowd.

The captain shrugs. 'If you don't need water or blankets, we can move on right away. Then I'll cancel the delivery.'

'Let's take a vote!' suggests a voice from the crowd.

The passengers carry out a show of hands. The decision to continue the journey is passed almost unanimously. The engine comes back to life.

Half an hour later, the ship sets course for Italy again. The sea grows rougher; mountains of water lift the boat aloft and drop it. Waves break across the prow, water runs below deck. Amal's clothes absorb the brine, growing heavy, wet and icy cold.

Fatima is asleep, her breathing soundless. The sleeping baby is no more than nine months old. Amal holds her in her arms – and here of all places, in the belly of the ship, she is overcome by an all-encompassing desire for her own child. The yearning is physical and hard to explain, except perhaps in the international language of pheromones. Amal knows now that she needs a baby, the tiny arms against her chest, the legs against her belly, the warm breath and the blind trust of which only an infant is capable.

The sea becomes more settled as morning approaches. A long queue forms outside the toilet, the only one for over seven hundred passengers. Amal and Youssef have stopped eating and drinking so they don't need to use it.

At noon the patched hole starts leaking and is welded shut again. The applause is less enthusiastic this time. They continue. But only a few hours later, an ominous black cloud appears in the sky. The wind picks up, double and then four times its previous strength. Fat drops of rain beat against the deck and then the storm breaks its bounds. The waves are ten metres high, rolling right across the ship. Lightning flashes out of the wall of cloud. The crew's movements become more hasty and urgent, the captain decides to turn back and wait out the storm between two Greek islands. The ship is tossed on the waves like a toy. Children squeal, old women scream at the tops of their voices. Men pass prayer beads between their fingers and the storm grows stronger. The ship is thrown upwards by a wave, rises above its foaming crest and descends seconds later into a trough. The deck is flooded with green water and white foam and the water leeches down to the inside of the ship. Then a wall of water looms before the prow and cascades down on them with elemental force. A loud, metallic boom passes through the ship's corpus but it doesn't break in two. The bad news: a transverse wave has crashed against the ship. And then comes another.

For three and a half hours, the crew manoeuvres the ship to the islands and somehow they actually make it all the way. The

Greek coastguard radios the captain – who assures the officer he's transporting salt from Greece to Croatia and only has to wait out the storm. But the coastguard doesn't trust him and a helicopter circles above the ship taking photos. The passengers have to stay hidden below deck and are told to put on their lifejackets, which Amal and Youssef do immediately. In the end the ship sets off again on an altered route, heading for Croatia to avert suspicion. The storm is still blowing but it's no longer life-threatening.

The captain steers the ship along the coastline. When he reaches Albanian waters he contacts the coastguard and confirms he's on his way to Croatia. Moments later, though, he changes course again, full speed ahead to Italy. The crew breaks off contact to the coastguard.

Towards noon, the sea now smooth as silk, the ship goes under. Its sinking is fast and unspectacular. People flee onto deck through the small hatch, only a few of them making it out in the crush. Those who possess lifejackets put them on and jump into the cold sea. Most of them can't swim.

Youssef is the first to reach the deck. Amal is behind him. Fatima hands her the baby, Amina, writhing and screaming. Then Fatima climbs out after Amal. Youssef and Amal drag her to the ship's rail but she grips it, not daring to jump. Youssef, however, leaps without hesitating. The ship is already listing, its stern now almost down to the water's surface. Amal too climbs over the rail and tries to pass the baby down to Youssef in the water as safely as she can. Once he has the child in his hands he swims as far away from the ship as possible.

Suddenly, the ship's weight shifts and the bow rises. People scream. Youssef signals to Amal to jump and at last she plummets into the sea, head-first.

The water surface feels like concrete, instantly pressing the air out of her lungs. Her throat and nose fill up with liquid. She sinks despite the lifejacket – which now proves to be a fake, absorbing water instead of keeping Amal afloat, dragging her down like a stone. Amal tries to struggle out of it, finally succeeding and kicking her way up to the surface.

Amal gasps for air. She barely has the strength to keep herself above water and she looks around for something to cling to. Parts of the wreck are floating on the surface, and other survivors too, calling desperately for help. Then she sees a lifejacket washed up without its owner, a genuine one. She swims over and grabs hold of it. Just as she's about to put it on, she sees Youssef in the distance. He still has hold of Amina and Amal struggles over to them, her energy spent. Youssef is overjoyed to see her. He says he thought she was dead and then he says he loves her.

They lay Amina on Amal's new lifejacket and keep talking to her to keep her awake. Amal clings to the float while Youssef, still wearing his vest, supports her from the other side, but her strength is waning. Amina keeps crying, Fatima is nowhere in sight and it seems to Amal that more and more people are going under. Amal hopes she'll die first; she couldn't stand to watch Youssef or the child drown.

'Help will be here soon,' Amal repeats over and over.

'Someone will have informed the coastguard,' Youssef says.

Amal and Youssef play with the baby, singing, but their voices tremble. A while later, no one can say when, another woman entrusts her child to Amal. It's a boy of about two. The woman doesn't have a lifejacket so Youssef gives her his. As he does so he returns Amal's gaze and whispers, 'I'm a good swimmer.' Amal wants to tell him not to give his lifejacket away anyway, but she can't.

Amal keeps the two children occupied as they sit side by side on the lifejacket. She does everything to stop them from falling asleep, recites counting rhymes, pulls faces, tickles their little bodies. But the children cry for their mothers. The adults' voices too sound more and more desperate. Despite the life-jacket, the boy's mother has drifted away, slowly. Amal doesn't have the strength to turn around to her. It's getting colder and colder, they haven't eaten properly for days and they can barely feel their limbs now. She could just close her eyes. She'd be at peace then. It would all be over at last.

'This is the Italian coastguard.' A few minutes or hours later, Amal can't tell, they hear amplified voices from far away. A helicopter circles above them, followed by rescue boats. They're red, inflatable dinghies bearing the words *Guardia Costiera*. Amal bursts into tears at the sight of them.

The Italian officers are wearing white protective suits, masks and plastic gloves to protect them from infection.

First they lift the boy and then the baby out of the water. They're both alive. Then Amal too feels herself pulled up. On board, she is wrapped in a warm blanket. She is taken to another, larger ship where she finds Amina and the boy again, also wrapped up warm. Youssef is with them too and Amal realizes she's experiencing the happiest moment in her life. They are taken to the infirmary.

A doctor examines the children. Amina starts crying in Amal's arms; Youssef tries to soothe her gently. The friendly paramedic asks Amal what her children's names are.

'Amina,' Youssef answers and then whispers, 'Amal, what on earth should we do?'

'And the boy?'

Amal gives him a confused look, only gradually realizing she's now responsible for two small children.

The doctor still has a friendly enquiring look on his face.

'Youssef?' Amal suggests, looking at the real Youssef.

'Nice name,' says the doctor.

The children are given milk to drink and fall asleep right away, exhausted. Amina is wrapped in a thick blanket, back in Amal's arms. The boy is asleep on Youssef's lap. Something about Youssef's touch surprises Amal; for the first time, she sees what tenderness he's capable of.

As soon as the ship docks, two Frontex officers embark to look for smugglers. As they leave the ship, Amal and Youssef hear a woman screaming behind them. Amal turns around and sees the little boy's mother fighting her way through the crowd, in tears. Youssef turns around too, beaming. The boy reaches out his tiny hands for his mother. The woman has reached them now and takes her child in her arms to the sound of sobs; her son, too, is crying and laughing at the same time.

On the shore, the immigration authority and aid workers await them. They are given a number to replace their identity from that point on. Amina is taken to hospital and examined there. She's released the next day with a clean bill of health.

In the meantime, Amal and Youssef have to undergo long interrogations. They now know there were more than seven hundred passengers on board their ship. Only three hundred survived. There's no trace of Amina's mother. The immigration officers all wear masks. Amal and Youssef are scared their story will be blown – they're scared Amina will be put in a home in Italy, and they're scared of looking like kidnappers. But the officers don't want to know anything about Amina, all they do is doubt Youssef and Amal's marital status.

The next day, a clapped-out bus takes them through the afternoon heat from the hospital to the reception centre, where they have to register. Amina sleeps against Amal's chest.

After survival comes bureaucracy. They're told they have to give a new form to their existence; refugees have to apply for asylum in the country where they first touch dry land in Europe, in their case Italy. But they have no documents any more – the sea destroyed Youssef's directing diploma, Amal's passport, their birth certificates and all the cash they had. The other refugees who've been in the camp for longer tell them they'll be deported immediately under the circumstances.

The camp itself is overcrowded, with people sleeping on floors or on tattered mattresses, the walls damp, the toilets blocked or non-existent, and the people's faces are so empty with hopelessness and apathy that Amal begs Youssef to escape. To anywhere.

The Italians are so overwhelmed by the new arrivals that the police officers don't look too closely, and so Youssef, Amal and Amina manage to simply sneak out of the camp.

They have neither money nor documents but they want to leave Italy as soon as possible and try to get to northern Europe, where their chances for asylum are better. Amal still has the jewellery she sewed into her bra but it seems impossible to sell it swiftly here in the Italian countryside. They walk to the nearest station and board a train. They fear ticket checks for the whole journey, hiding in the toilet, but no one comes. At Milan, they get off the train.

The main station is crowded with refugees. A young Syrian man lends Amal his phone and she logs into Facebook and calls her brother. To her surprise, he picks up. His voice sounds as carefree as ever while tears run down Amal's cheeks.

'Ali, I need your help,' she says.

'Are you still in Beirut?'

'No, in Milan.'

'What are you doing there?'

'It's a long story but I... I mean we, we have to get out of here. Ali, can you send me some money?'

'I'll go straight to Western Union.'

'I'll pay you back.'

'Don't worry.'

'No, I really will pay you back.'

'Amal, try to get to Germany. I'll wait for you there.'

'Where?'

'Berlin.'

'I'll call you again.'

'The money's on its way.'

The young man accompanies them to a branch of Western Union a few hours later, where they collect several hundred euro against the stranger's ID. Then they go to a department store – they need new clothes so as not to stand out.

The bright lights, the music, the make-up displays, the buzz of voices and the pushy saleswomen are too much for them. Amal chooses a dress and buys it without trying it on, and gets vests, babygros, a hat and a jacket, nappies, bottles, formula, a rattle and a blanket for Amina; Youssef has to manage with cheap jeans and a white T-shirt.

They leave the store as quickly as they can, heading straight for the station.

The train to Munich doesn't leave for an hour so they have no choice but to sit down in a McDonald's. Amal mixes formula with warm water and feeds Amina as Youssef eats a Big Mac meal. They're still doubting their decision to keep the child but they agree it's probably best for her if she stays with them for the time being. Once they get to the north they'll try to find Amina's family. She might have grandmothers, aunts, uncles or cousins who are still alive.

The pain comes suddenly. Amal runs to the toilet, locks the door, sits down and waits for everything to come pouring out of her. Her stomach cramps up and she's glad she's here and not on the Mediterranean. Bent double, she sits on the toilet seat, crying. Once it's all over and she thinks she can get up, she leaves the cubicle. As she soaps her hands at the washbasin she studies her reflection. She doesn't recognize herself. Her cheeks have collapsed, her eyes are deep in their sockets.

The city sinks in a sandstorm. A huge, dirty cloud of sand rolls slowly along the ground, burying everything in its course. It resembles an ancient mountain range, sprung up overnight. The dust worms its way into every nook and cranny in every house and into every lung.

Even before Hammoudi decides to leave, Naji has contacted the smuggler. He collects him barely an hour later. It's the same man who took him to Turkey, which appeases Hammoudi. Only now is he certain he'll really be leaving Deir ez-Zor. Naji has given him money for his escape, which he hides beneath his clothing. The smuggler drives right up to the hospital and Little Man brings Hammoudi out on a stretcher, wrapped in white shrouds. The smuggler heaves him into the boot of his car. He offers to take Little Man along too, but Little Man decides to stay. He and Hammoudi say their goodbyes with a long hug.

The sandstorm means visibility is down to only a few inches, so they drive at walking pace to the village of Abu Khashab, once known for its good wheat and now one of the few places that have not yet fallen to Daesh. The villagers are supporters of the revolution, still willing to help the people-smugglers. Hammoudi feels like he's suffocating. He tries to stay awake but the dust is everywhere.

Half an hour later, Hammoudi is able to leave the boot inside a dark garage, and switches to the front seat of a different car. There are two former Red Crescent helpers on the back seat, and a photographer. All of them have to leave Syria as quickly as possible.

They take dirt tracks to the settlement of Al-Alyad and reach Tall Abyad near the border seven hours later. They're usually waved straight through at the checkpoints as they come from the villages and not the cities, and even when they are stopped they soon set off again. All five of them try to look untroubled and harmless.

They leave the car near the border crossing. Their smuggler takes his leave and returns to Syria's interior. In his place comes a man who walks them to the border and then to Akçakale on the Turkish side.

Only an hour later, Hammoudi is loaded into another car and that evening is let out in Gaziantep. Dazzled by the lights, he stumbles through the streets as though drunk. At some point he walks into a hotel and asks for a room. He's handed a key and taken to the second floor by the porter. The room is decorated with some abandon, the furniture painted glossy white with golden detail; the carpet is worn and brown, just like the curtains, which smell of smoke; the sheets on the bed are in clashing colours.

The first thing Hammoudi does is run a bath, and the hot running water shocks him as much as all the lights in the city. After his bath he falls into a long and dreamless sleep.

Waking up hours later, he looks at the old-fashioned telephone on the bedside table. It's dark green, all the numbers on it rubbed away. Not until he hears her voice on the other end is Hammoudi aware that he's automatically dialled Claire's number.

'Yes?' she says.

'It's Hammoudi.'

She doesn't reply.

'Shall I hang up?' he asks.

'No.' Hammoudi thinks he detects a hint of panic in Claire's voice. 'It's just... Jesus, Hammoudi, I thought you were dead,' he hears her sob.

'Claire, I've got out.'

'I was certain you were dead! You didn't get in touch, other-wise I'd have…'

'It's fine, really it is. I've got out now.' The line crackles; Hammoudi closes his eyes to understand Claire better.

'Out where?'

'I'm in Turkey.'

'Are you alright?'

'Yes. How are you? What's the weather like in Paris?'

'Hammoudi, what the hell?'

'I don't know what to say, sorry.'

'Are you really alright?'

'I'm alive.'

'I waited for you.'

'Claire, I could come back, I could come home.'

'You don't understand, Hammoudi.'

'What?'

'I have a child now.'

'Is it mine?'

'For God's sake, no. Hammoudi…'

Hammoudi hangs up and starts pacing the brown carpet. The phone rings; it must be Claire calling him back. He knows he couldn't expect her to wait four years for him. They never made any agreement. And yet he still clung to a hope to which he had no right. Hammoudi answers the telephone.

'Hello, this is reception. We just wanted to say we'll have to charge the long-distance call to your credit card.'

'I don't have a credit card.'

'I see. Would you please come down, then?'

Hammoudi is standing on the shore, watching a simple black dinghy being inflated with a small pump that looks like a toy. The passengers are busy packing their documents, medications and a small amount of jewellery into watertight balloons. Hammoudi got himself a crossing in Izmir. After talking to Claire he'd wanted to stay in Turkey, where his parents and sister are living, but they told him he had to leave the country – Daesh men had paid a visit to their house in Mardin and asked after Hammoudi.

Nervous, he smokes one cigarette after another. Next to him, a man in a tatty, brown leather jacket is also smoking as though his life depended on it. He has big brown eyes ringed by deep black shadows, bushy eyebrows and a large Roman nose. To judge by his accent, he's Iraqi. Hammoudi offers him one of his cigarettes. The man introduces himself as Mohammed.

The two of them watch the smugglers in silence as they patrol the beach in small, armed groups. Their boat is the last of eight; the others set off for Greece the previous day. The smugglers held their boat up at the last minute and ordered them to wait overnight near the coast. Fifty-odd people tried to get some rest on a forest floor, without blankets or any kind of bedding.

One smuggler, a small man with warts on his face and a heavy Palestinian accent, gives instructions, and for a brief moment there's a shimmer of normality – the traffickers are acting exactly like flight attendants on a scheduled flight. Perhaps this is simply the new reality. 'If you see the Turkish coastguard, do nothing, they'll take you back to Turkey. Nothing will happen to you. If you see the Greek coastguard they'll destroy your boat, but they'll take you safely to Greece.' The smugglers' instructions are clear.

A little boy with a mane of dark curls and blue eyes stares at Hammoudi and then asks, 'Are we going to die?'

Hammoudi swallows and then tries to inject confidence into his voice as he answers. 'No.'

'Can you do anything?'

Hammoudi shakes his head.

'You know, it's alright if we die, I just don't want to go back,' the boy says.

The boat – designed for eight passengers – is loaded with fifty people. Children cling to their parents in panic. Two older women, one of them lame, adopt stoic expressions. As more and more people climb into the boat, one woman cracks and screams that there are too many, they'll all go under. The trafficker, unimpressed, raises his gun in a gesture of indulgent superiority: an HK33 automatic rifle, made in Germany, Heckler & Koch. But the boat really is too full; everyone has to leave their bags behind.

The smuggler explains they'll now be heading in a straight line to a Greek island, not telling them its name. He doesn't get into the boat but tugs it out to sea behind his white jet-ski. His face is as relaxed as a holidaymaker's. The outboard motor is entrusted to a young man. The only thing that qualified him for the job was the fact that he used to clean refrigerated containers at a harbour; he's never seen the inside of a ship. He gets the crossing for free in return for navigating the boat – but he also bears the greatest risk. He's responsible for fifty lives and he could be arrested for trafficking.

The men sit around the outside edge with the women and

children crouched in the middle, slightly more protected. Separated from the water only by the thin plastic beneath them, they're all instantly soaked through by the spray. The wind is icy and there's nothing for them to hold onto. People pray to God. They don't even pray to arrive safely, only to die with their families. Parents hope they won't survive their children.

No one speaks to begin with, only the Iraqi who has squeezed in next to Hammoudi cursing quietly to himself. Hammoudi looks up at the star-studded sky and tries not to think of Deir ez-Zor and his patients. He'd rather think of the stars and how they've been extinguished, even though their light still reaches the earth. He gazes at the constellations, trying to remember their names. Dawn arrives gradually and the sun rises as a red ball of fire.

A little girl, perhaps eight years old, with freckles and two dark plaits resting on her luminous lifejacket, suddenly screams at the top of her voice and points at three fins protruding from the water. She keeps repeating a word that must mean 'sharks' in Kurdish. Her face is wet with tears. Several women also start screaming as if on command, and the men would like to join in but are embarrassed to do so.

'They're only dolphins,' Hammoudi tries to reassure the girl, but the whole boat is talking and yelling.

As the first rays of the new day's sun fall upon the boat, an island appears ahead of them – not far away at all. Hammoudi and the Iraqi try to make jokes to stop the children from being scared, but the island is no closer even two hours later. Hammoudi can't help feeling the sea is expanding.

He can barely feel his hunger now. It's only his thirst that troubles him. His lips are cracked and his mouth is dry, his swollen tongue making it hard to breathe.

At noon, they spot the lighthouse at the northern end of Lesbos, and they also see the lifeguards in orange vests on the beach, pointing the way for them. Some are about to jump into the water, but one lifeguard shouts in English and then in broken Arabic, 'English, English, who speaks English?' The Iraqi puts his hand up and translates the man's words into Arabic: 'Don't worry! We're not the police! Switch off the motor and sit down. Don't jump out of the boat, it's dangerous!' The helpers now guide the boat to a makeshift landing platform. A human chain takes first the babies, then the toddlers and the older children, then the two old women, who look very relieved, then they help the remaining women and finally the men. The whole thing goes quickly and routinely. Hammoudi is startled though when he gets out of the boat – the rocks have sharp edges and it hurts to put pressure on his legs; they threaten to slip away beneath him.

Their boat has hardly arrived before the locals start gathering, barely waiting for the refugees to disembark. Boats that land on Lesbos are taken apart immediately – the first to go is the motor, then the rudder and even the plastic sheets, which are used on farms for animals or for collecting olives.

As soon as the people are on dry land, they cast off their lifejackets in joy. They thank the volunteers and calm down their children, now crying and trembling with cold. Some try to get a phone connection to let their relatives know they've survived. Their faces are radiant with hope. Naïve about the future.

Hammoudi too is given a thermal blanket and exchanges his shoes and clothes for dry ones. The volunteers gather up the soaked clothing, which they will wash and bring back to the beach for the next new arrivals.

After a while, a bus comes to pick them up. They are taken to Camp Moria, a former prison.

The facilities consist of stuffy white container units and a sea of tents alongside the actual camp, which is sealed off with barbed wire. It is dusty and the inhabitants' faces speak of absolute exhaustion. The containers are full and Hammoudi is allowed to buy a tent. An entire commercial district has sprung up around the camp: an improvised taxi rank, mobile-charging stations and kiosks selling water, biscuits and tents. Hammoudi decides against spending money on a tent. He hopes to move on that night. The size of the camp and the newly created logistics amaze him, and he involuntarily observes the scene through an ethnologist's eyes.

Illegal immigration is strictly regimented at the camp, though not by the European governments. There's a hierarchy of refugees. Syrians usually arrive in whole families and in boats that are slightly better and not quite as overcrowded. They're from the former middle class and they have small financial reserves that have enabled them to get to Europe. Pakistanis and Afghans cross the Mediterranean in extremely unseaworthy boats, in some cases so tightly packed that they don't even have space to sit.

The Afghans are also the best prepared for their journey – their rucksacks are very well packed and they often have instant access to dry shoes and socks. Syrians, though, often don't have a plan, they don't know what's happening to them. The preparedness of its emigrants is still the best indicator of the state of a society. At the bottom of the hierarchy are the people from central and northern Africa.

Queuing for initial registration, Hammoudi bumps into the Iraqi from the boat. He's glad of a familiar face and Mohammed feels the same way. They stay together from that point on. There's not much to do; all that's demanded of them is to hold out. They have to wait overnight for their turn to register.

As dusk draws in, a small fire is lit; people warm their feet and hands and eat tinned tuna and bread. The fire hisses. Hammoudi and Mohammed spend the night under the stars with others. Someone keeps the fire burning with pieces of wood. They tell each other nothing, saying nothing about their escape, their countries, their wars, their wives, their children, their houses or their futures. Too great is the fear of the all-powerful security services.

By first light, the fire has burned out.

Towards noon, the refugees are allowed to move on. Their route takes them a whole day on foot across the island, but they don't mind. For Hammoudi and the Iraqi, it has been a long time since they last moved around legally – and they know it will be the last time in a while. So they decide to enjoy their walk, a little at least.

They cross a forest, climb a mountain and then walk back down again, always following the narrow country road, past olive trees and cypresses, high grass, occasional houses with brightly painted shutters and ivory-coloured walls. They admire the view of the cliffs along the coastline and they see the sea, its crowns of foam and the rough furrows carved into the water's surface by the wind.

They talk about where they want their journey to take them. Everything seems possible: Finland, Sweden, Germany or the Netherlands. All they have to do is evade the police.

Mohammed has left his family behind in Iraq and is determined to make it to northern Europe, to Sweden or perhaps to Britain; only there does he stand a chance of bringing the family together quickly. His wife is pregnant again. He probably won't see the child until it's started walking. He takes out his mobile phone and shows Hammoudi photos of his daughters.

At Mytilene harbour, they wait beneath the glaring sun for a ferry to Athens. Tourists stare at them, unabashed. Hammoudi wonders when he last saw so many unharmed bodies.

The ferry is huge, especially in comparison to the tiny inflatable dinghy by which they arrived in Europe illegally two nights ago. The final preparations are under way, the metal boarding ramps let down. Vehicles start their engines and drive on board. The foot passengers follow them.

Almost everyone on the ferry is an immigrant; overwrought and overtired with children whining and whinging. Hammoudi wonders why it's so easy now. Why he couldn't just get on a ferry straight to Lesbos and donate the other 1,290 euros to the German or Swedish state.

As soon as they get to Athens they try to head further north. They make it to the Greece–Macedonia border, cross it full of fear and then travel on towards Serbia. That leads to the absurd situation of having to leave the EU again to get further north. Helped by other refugees who provide them with key information about the various routes, they finally make it to Serbia.

They try to sleep on the trains in which they spend a couple of hours without changing, but they can't get a moment's rest because their fear of the police keeps them awake. Time becomes a geographical specification, measurable only in terms of the distance to the next border or the next town. They lose track of the days of the week and Google Maps routes flicker behind their eyelids when they close their eyes. They're in a permanent state of fear. Their bodies are constantly on the alert.

Mohammed and Hammoudi spend several days in Belgrade, where it rains relentlessly and is bitterly cold. Without papers they can find no shelter, neither in hostels nor in hotels. If they slept on the street or in a shop doorway they'd risk getting picked up by the police. So they wander the city aimlessly and hope that something will happen.

At some point, a man approaches them and asks whether they need accommodation. His eyes are far apart, his features crude. He suggests they sleep in his living room, for twenty euros each; they can take a shower and even stay for twelve hours, he says, and then the next people will be coming. They agree.

The flat is small and warm. For Mohammed and Hammoudi, it's the first real flat they've been in for a long time. Two camping mats are rolled out on the living room floor and then they take turns in the shower. Their host even makes them a thick lentil soup in the evening, with roughly cut bread. The warmth and comfort bring tears to their eyes.

The next day, they take a slow train to the Hungarian border and get out in the last Serbian village. They stock up on bread, tinned fish and bottled water. Mohammed leaves a voice message for his wife.

The border runs along the middle of a forest, where they're told it's easier to cross. But the forest has its dangers too – there are stubborn rumours of criminal gangs hiding in the woods to rob refugees and even remove their organs. Suffering is a hard currency.

Hammoudi and Mohammed join a group of five friends from Damascus who grew up on the same street and have known each other all their lives. They have to pass through the forest alone – the smugglers are waiting for them on the other side of the border.

Their only protection is the long sticks each of them holds. Dusk is already settling in. Hammoudi breaks out in a sweat.

They move as quietly and inconspicuously as possible, but then they spot police officers in full combat gear running towards them, some way off. Not knowing what to do, the men run into the woods. The trees are tall and dark. They hope to blend into the thicket. They hear dogs barking in the distance; they must be police dogs. They see fallen trees giving way to a small clearing and they run to the darkest spot, taking care not to stumble over exposed roots. Hammoudi feels his own heartbeat. They have to climb trees, get as high among the branches as they can. Hammoudi's hands tremble but he makes it up somehow. His arms are scraped open, his trembling gets stronger and stronger. The leaves rustle in the wind. He was never scared during the bombings in Syria. Instead, he'd try to estimate the number of victims brought in and pray there wouldn't be too many hopeless cases. Here, there's nothing to distract him from his own fate.

The young man in the tree next to Hammoudi's has a panic attack. He hyperventilates and his breathing is painful, but nobody helps him. They can't even talk to him to calm him down, for fear of being discovered. Suddenly, the police call off the dogs. Mohammed whispers to the others, 'Don't climb down, it's a trap.' The forest grows very quiet, even the leaves no longer rustling.

They spend another hour motionless in the trees, until Mohammed jumps down, followed by Hammoudi and then the others. They tread cautiously, creeping from one bush to the next, taking care not to leave their cover.

Hammoudi thinks he hears dogs barking and he signals to them all to lie flat on the ground. They hear the border guards coming closer. Branches break and dogs growl. They're surrounded.

'Don't move!' voices call out.

They don't move a muscle. Hammoudi feels the barrel of a gun on the back of his head, sees dirty boots, even smells them and their dogs. The policemen have them encircled, laughing and yelling, and they force the men to their feet. When Hammoudi stands up a blow hits the backs of his knees and he collapses again. He hears a weak moan next to him, no doubt from someone in his group. Hammoudi tries to turn around but a policeman grabs his head and forces him to the ground. Another takes a step towards them, opens his flies and takes out his penis, which is small, red and uncircumcised. A warm liquid hits Hammoudi's face; he clenches his eyes and lips shut and hears the other man holding onto him bellow into his ear, 'You immigrant cunt.'

Their group is led to the next clearing and lined up. A German shepherd is ready to pounce, its hackles raised in a furious growl. The highest-ranking officer accepts the money. He looks cheerful and inspects his prisoners with curiosity, as if to say, don't take it personally, I like hummus too. Once he's pocketed the cash all the policemen and the dog withdraw.

Hammoudi, Mohammed and the others stay put in the clearing. None of them says a word. Eventually they set off to leave the woods as fast as they can. Shortly afterwards, Hammoudi and Mohammed find their smuggler at the agreed meeting place, change their clothes and cross the border with no further difficulties. They take their leave from the five friends, who don't trust traffickers and don't want to spend money on them.

PART III

By the time they arrive in Berlin it's autumn. The leaves turn greenish yellow and then the yellow grows deeper, changes to golden yellow, orange, vermillion, carmine and finally crimson. People sit outside cafés and restaurants trying to catch the last rays of sun, though they no longer warm properly and everything will soon be immersed in drab grey. The days grow shorter again, the air grows colder.

The waiting room at the central reception point for refugees is crowded and stuffy. People of all origins sit and wait. Children whine, babies cry, but their mothers barely have the strength to soothe them.

Youssef and Amal have to wait. They don't know what for, but the whys are gradually losing all meaning anyway. The German authorities' waiting rooms, hopelessly overcrowded, the staff chronically overworked and shuffling exasperatingly slowly along the corridors, plunge the waiting people first into paralysis and then into agitation. They each expect their own number to finally light up on the LED panel at any moment, but this expectation is soon followed by the frustration of realizing that every number takes up at least half an hour's processing, and then replaced by pure rage, strong enough to drive tears to the eyes of grown women and men. Amal and Youssef have waited outside and inside from three in the morning until late afternoon, from eight in the morning until closing time, and each time they were missing either a document or a piece of information, meaning they always had to come back again.

They're telling the authorities they're a family. Amina is getting Youssef's surname; only the missing papers are causing problems. Now they're to take a language test to establish whether they're Syrian. Ali tries to help them, assuring the authorities Amal is his sister, but he gradually withdraws, eventually only contacting them sporadically.

Their tiny room in the asylum seekers' home contains an old cot, and they spend the last of the money borrowed from Amal's brother on a changing mat and more baby clothes, which Amina grows out of at an astonishing speed. They go to a paediatrician, who assures them the baby is healthy. Her new parents hope she'll forget the crossing. Perhaps they also secretly hope she'll forget her mother. All their attempts to track down her relatives have failed. There seems to be no one who knows Fatima or her husband. No one is looking for Amina.

Amal feels guilty – the child she so coveted has become hers. She feels as though it was her longing that killed the mother, as if she'd robbed the child of her real mother through her insolent wish and now she'll fail as a mother herself. She'll always be just a poor substitute, she fears, will never be good enough for this child. Amal presses Amina closer to her chest.

Youssef, Amal and the baby leave the office and go to a street café for a brief rest. They order only one coffee, which they share between them, and hot milk for Amina. They can't afford more than that. Amal watches the women passing by on the street. Different women, well dressed and beautiful women, with long sleek hair or smart short cuts. Women in expensive dresses and high heels. Women on bikes, women with buggies, women with full shopping bags, women rushing somewhere, women stopping to look at shop windows. Suddenly Amal realizes she's no longer one of them. Nobody takes any notice of her now. Where is her house? Her career? And her street that always smelled of jasmine? Where is the ironed and folded laundry from her chests of drawers? Where are her evening dresses and her father's shirts, fresh from the dry cleaners? Where are her books and records? Where are her friends and relatives? The parties and summers around the pool? Where are the complicated film shoots and the exhausting rehearsals at the theatre?

Amal hates moving around the city as a refugee – hesitant and frightened. She hates her entire existence. She hates not being able to speak German and the way no one in the municipal authorities other than the security guards is capable of speaking even basic English. She hates being seen as a Muslim and a scrounger and she hates herself. The world has invented a new race – the race of refugees, *Flüchtlinge*, Muslims or newcomers. The condescension is palpable in every breath.

Suddenly, Youssef says, 'The revolution was a mistake.'

'Are you joking?' Amal asks.

Youssef starts speaking, hesitant at first and then faster and faster. 'Even if Assad falls, nothing will change in Syria any time soon. The regime has inscribed itself upon us. You can find the next dictator every five metres in every prison in the country. There was only one mattress in my group cell and there was a fat man sitting on it and giving orders. Imagine it. Five men sat around him to protect him from the others' lice. They had this chemical spray from somewhere, and they sprayed it on us every two hours. We, the ten of us who had lice, had to spend our days next to the toilet, although toilet's an exaggeration for that hole in the ground. We had our own leader too, because we weren't allowed to address the boss directly, we had to speak to our leader first and then he'd decide whether our words were worth passing on. Every group had one.'

Amal stares at him, not understanding, and Youssef explains. 'We were divided into five groups. The first one was the boss and his bodyguards, then came those who had someone in prison to watch over them, the third was the men who were vaguely clean and had money on them when they were arrested. Then came all the foreigners they couldn't expel, Pakistanis, Algerians and so on. And then there was us, of course. We had to stand up whenever someone wanted to use the toilet. They'd beat us if we weren't quick enough. In fact the boss's gang was always beating someone or other. Once they brought a crack addict into us. He was trembling all over and in dire need of medication, but the boss ordered his men to beat him and put a plastic bag over his head. After two days of that, the crack addict went crazy and then the boss changed his mind – he wanted to keep him as his dog and pat him, and the bodyguards tripped over themselves to prove their love. They cut his fingernails, kissed his forehead, massaged his feet. How is democracy supposed to work with people like that, tell me? Remember how everyone in Syria dreamed of having power and joining the secret service? Just like we always tried to be friends with at least one government man, to be on the safe side? Like your friend Luna? We all paid our generals lavishly, gave them presents and did everything so they wouldn't send us packing when we needed their favours one day.'

Amal stares at Youssef in horror. 'And what has Luna got to do with all that?'

'Your best friend is the daughter of a man devoted to the regime! She is the regime! You still haven't cut her out of your life!'

'You want me to unfriend her on Facebook or what? What do you expect of me?'

'Nothing. I expect nothing at all of you.'

Amal gets up and goes to the window. It's still raining. She wishes she could leave Youssef. But what would become of Amina? Amal is scared he'd take her away from her.

'Youssef, we can't go on like this, you and me.'

'I know.' Youssef joins Amal at the window. 'I'm sorry,' he says and puts an arm around her waist, but at that moment Amina wakes up and demands their attention.

Not until they reached Germany did Hammoudi and Mohammed encounter the police. They were on a train, not far from Frankfurt am Main, where they were planning to part ways. Hammoudi was heading for France and Mohammed to Sweden, when two police officers set out to check the train. Hammoudi gave himself up voluntarily while Mohammed hid in the toilet. He actually made it all the way. Weeks later, Mohammed sent Hammoudi a Facebook message and thanked him for enabling him to continue to Sweden. He was now living in a refugee camp in the northernmost part of the country, waiting for his refugee status to be recognized so that his family could join him. He hoped it wouldn't take much longer. He was trying to learn Swedish, he wrote.

Hammoudi, meanwhile, embarks on an odyssey from the Frankfurt reception centre for refugees to a holding centre in Bavaria, then another near Düsseldorf and the next in Dresden, before landing up in Berlin because there's no space anywhere else. There, he gets a room in a hostel, shared with five other men. Two of them are from Chechnya, two from Iran and one from Sri Lanka. They can't even wish each other good night. They all snore. There are bags under their beds that haven't been unpacked since they left their homes. They spend all day waiting for something to happen, enviously eyeing the tourists who are free, allowed to travel, study and work. The hostel is still running normally, except that the refugees aren't permitted to eat their meals with the other guests. There's one floor for tourists and one for refugees.

The hardest thing for Hammoudi is never being alone. In the dining hall, in the bedroom, in the shared bathroom and even in the corridors there are people who don't know what to do with themselves. He can't sleep at night; that's when the memories surface that he's tried to block out.

By day he explores the city on foot, sets off without a map or a plan, takes his bearings from the main roads, reconnoitres side streets and whole neighbourhoods. He thinks Berlin is ugly, everything flat, the architecture unimaginative and the people badly dressed. It's a city for provincial teenagers with no cares in the world. Hammoudi has to stop himself from constantly comparing Berlin to Paris. He's still planning to move on to France, but he won't be allowed until his asylum case is closed. That's fine by him. Picking up his old life in Paris seems impossible right now.

It takes weeks before he finally gets an appointment for his hearing. He's to turn up in an obscure place near the edge of town at eight in the morning.

There, he finds a box-shaped building with a single waiting room that smells of stale air, poverty and sweat. Outside, men in tracksuit bottoms are smoking. Hammoudi joins them and asks them for a light. The sky is obscured by clouds. Someone new joins them every ten minutes. Hour after hour passes. The waiting room fills up, people spread out across the corridors, the stairwell and the courtyard.

Hammoudi's name is called at two o'clock. He follows a short woman into an office where two people are waiting for him, a huge mountain of a woman and a younger man. The caseworker gives him a gentle smile. She has framed pictures of her children on her desk, all three with dark brown curls and blue eyes. Hammoudi feels he can trust her.

Through the interpreter, the caseworker tells Hammoudi she's now ready to hear his story. The interpreter is Egyptian and despite all the Egyptian soaps his mother used to watch in the kitchen, Hammoudi has difficulty understanding his dialect.

'Do you speak French?' he asks the caseworker.

'Yes, but not enough,' she answers in an impeccable accent, and continues in German. The interpreter glares at Hammoudi and translates that he should start now, please. Hammoudi is suddenly uncertain and remembers nothing. His story suddenly seems to him like a fairy tale. Does he even have a story? He's not sure any more. Where should he start? He remembers his parents' house, surrounded by peaceful silence in the early morning. There was a teahouse opposite where old men used to play backgammon.

The woman gives an expectant cough. He looks her in the eye and tries to gauge whether she's capable of extending sympathy towards him.

Hammoudi takes a deep breath and begins. 'I was born in Saudi Arabia in 1980 – my parents had been working there as primary school teachers. I was ten when we returned to Syria. We lived in Deir ez-Zor.'

'Where is that?'

'Not far from the border with Iraq. I went to school there. Then I started university but it took me a long time to find the right course. I ended up doing medicine.'

'Did you study in Deir ez-Zor?'

'No, in Paris.'

The case worker looks surprised.

'I had a grant and I wanted to stay there, but the Syrian regime withdrew my exit visa.'

'When was that?'

'2011.'

'And then?'

'Then the revolution broke out.'

He looks his caseworker directly in the eye for a moment. Then he goes on hastily, speaks for a whole hour, the caseworker taking notes and not interrupting him. It's the first time Hammoudi has told anyone about the past four years of his life, the first time he's had an opportunity to order the events in his mind and reflect on them. After two hours, he's free to go. He thanks the woman and closes the door behind him, quietly.

Settling in takes a long time and isn't easy. Amal and Youssef struggle through the asylum process and the German course, and then Youssef finds a job in an Arabic supermarket. The work frustrates him but he's too despondent to look for anything else. Amal doesn't have any work but she's signed up with an acting agency. She applied without a recommendation, just with her CV, photos and a few video clips, and they put her on their books. When she signed her contract it felt briefly as though her life might be moving forwards, but no job has ever come out of it.

One day her phone rings and the assistant to her agent, a man she's never met, suggests auditioning for a cooking show. The assistant claims it's perfect for Amal.

'Over my dead body,' Amal answers.

Still, she notes down the date and the address for the casting. The concept is apparently to present dishes from countries roughly grouped together under the term 'unsafe third countries'. The working title is *Refugees Can Cook Too*.

When she tells Youssef about the casting that evening he laughs long and hard. They're sitting at their small kitchen table, both labouring over their German homework.

'What would you cook?' Youssef asks.

'Hummus,' says Amal, folding her arms.

'No, seriously, what would your concept be?' Youssef asks.

'The concept's already set in stone.'

'And what is it?'

'They want *exotic Middle Eastern* food.'

'Okay, then hummus.'

'I'm not going to do the job. I still make so many mistakes in my spoken German.'

'That could be the whole point.' Youssef tries to provoke Amal, saying, 'But I don't know what they'd like about your cooking.'

'That's it, Youssef! I'm never cooking for you again.'

'But then I'd starve to death!' Youssef makes a show of regret, getting up from his chair and going over to kiss Amal. He puts his right hand on her neck and is just about to place his other hand strategically on Amal's breast when Amina starts to cry in the bedroom.

'I'll go,' Youssef murmurs.

For the first time in her life, Amal reluctantly begins watching cooking shows. She even likes some of them. She soon finds out that the meals they make aren't actually the main thing. It's all about lifestyle concepts and marketing oneself. Most of the niches are already occupied, though.

The first audition is held in a spacious converted factory loft in Kreuzberg. A kitchen island has been set up in the middle of the room and the applicants, twenty recently arrived young women of non-specific ethnic descent, have fifteen minutes each to prepare a small dish in front of the camera and tell their life story while they're at it.

When Amal's turn comes she conjures up her father's restaurant. Her story ends with his other family. She doesn't even wait to find out how it went, leaving the set in a rage at herself.

The next day, she's invited to more test shoots and a trial cooking session. Even though she doesn't want the job, Amal now starts fighting for it. She goes through the shelves of cookbooks in the local library. Then she strolls through the supermarkets with Amina in her buggy, in search of the best ingredients for her menu. Amina burbles away happily and waves at other babies, although she never pays them as much attention as dogs or cats.

They've hinted that Amal may well get a contract, so she takes a far-too-short dress out of the wardrobe and puts on lipstick. A little bit of red rubs off on her white teeth.

The associate producer is a man named Matthias, but he's recently been calling himself Matthew in an attempt to appear worldlier. He's insisted on showing Amal his kitchen; apparently, it's worthy of a Michelin-starred restaurant.

Matthew's house is in an area that exudes affluence – Amal passes private kindergartens and multilingual primary schools. The front gardens are well kept and spacious, the houses flooded with light, their inhabitants white and slim.

As she enters Matthew's living room she notices not only the soft rugs, the fireplace and the rustic wooden table, but also the family photos showing a blonde woman with a pageboy haircut and stick-thin arms hugging two laughing boys. Alongside them is a Christmas tree, sparsely decorated with a few wooden toys. Matthew sees Amal looking and hurries her through.

'Come on, let me show you my kitchen,' he says.

The kitchen looks expensive and overblown, the surfaces all granite and brushed steel. Amal thinks of her own kitchen in Damascus and is surprised to feel tears pricking her eyes. Matthew has a stove with eight hotplates, all of which look unused, and an ambitiously oversized fridge, and Amal spots a *sous vide* machine out of the corner of her eye.

She's learned by now that people in the West consume only symbols. At her third casting session, she served artichokes with foie gras and poularde demi-deuil – with truffles under the skin – to signal that she's perfectly capable of pleasing sophisticated tastes. As she sliced the truffles and inserted them under the poularde's skin, she talked to the camera about Middle Eastern cuisine, a very natural way of cooking without artificial flavourings, saying her mother only used the best products at home, all grown and produced locally. For dessert, she served a chocolate cake with a liquid centre and home-made ice cream. Bassel taught her the chicken recipe when she was little, the cake was out of a packet and the ice cream came from the nearest supermarket, but as they'd overrun their recording time the crew simply ate it all up and no one took any notice of the preparation.

Matthew had quickly speculated that the show might be generously supported by a large chain of organic supermarkets, so Amal had to adjust her appearance to fit the image of the potential advertising client: not too much make-up, her hair mid-length and curly, her clothes understated and expensive. But they couldn't do without certain Orientalist touches – she always wore striking jewellery referred to as *ethnic*, usually from Dolce & Gabbana. The jewellery and clothes were provided by a stylist; after the shoot they were neatly packed in boxes and sent back to the relevant company.

Now Matthew's standing in his kitchen, little boy lost, his shirt slightly too tight with too many buttons undone. A few droplets of sweat on his forehead compete for shininess with the subtle tan of a man who goes sailing regularly. He pours himself a glass of wine and degusts it, his lips giving off a sound Amal finds almost unbearably embarrassing. She tries to keep the annoyance off her face. Once he's finally swallowed, he pours her a glass too. She drinks soundlessly.

'This is my Pacojet. I use it to make Michelin-standard ice cream, but I did have to raid the old piggy bank for it.'

'Did your wife not mind?'

Matthew pretends not to have heard the question. 'It's a limited edition.' He tries to brush Amal's elbow but she shakes his hand off.

'And this is my Salamander. Adjustable-height grill. Excellent!' he exclaims, shoving Amal ahead of him to admire another appliance.

'You know,' he says to her after they've eaten a mediocre meal and while he's serving crème brûlée with beetroot as dessert, 'I refer to myself as gastrosexual.'

Amal breathes a sigh of relief.

He reads her face and rushes to add, 'Not homosexual, gastrosexual. There's nothing wrong with men cooking. Women cook what they can, men cook what they want.'

After dessert, Amal swiftly makes her excuses and flees the scene.

To her great surprise, she receives a contract in the post a few days later. For the pilot episode, she made several Syrian dishes and promised the viewers a trip back in time to an unharmed Syria. As mezze, she made tuna on taboule salad, the tuna marinated in advance, then a few quick recipes like mutabbal, aubergine purée with tahini, fried aubergines with feta cheese and green salad. The main course was roast chicken in lemon-and-thyme sauce. Amal rubbed the chicken with plenty of garlic and a paste made of salt, sumach, lemon zest, fresh thyme leaves and a little olive oil.

The pilot has proved a big success. It seems the bored housewives of the Western world have been waiting all this time for Amal and her exotic cuisine.

Amal is in the kitchen with Amina, the room filled with the scent of sautéed onions, and the baby is peering curiously into the cast iron pan. They moved into their own flat a few months ago. It was difficult to find a place; hardly anyone wanted to rent to refugees, let alone refugees with a toddler. Once they'd got used to the disappointments, an aid organization helped them find a small one-bedroom flat.

They should be happy but they aren't. The atmosphere between Amal and Youssef has become more and more strained, they've moved further and further apart, and if it hadn't been for the shared secret of Amina's origins they would have separated long ago.

Amal's work as a TV chef doesn't make her happy. She comes home at night exhausted and gets up tired at dawn, a little more frustrated each day.

When Amal is at home, she spends most of her time in the kitchen. When she's cooking she conjures up memories, not just her own but those of the people who taught her how to make each dish, and those of the generations before them.

Suddenly something shifts inside her. She reaches for the telephone and dials Ali's number.

'Did you know about the other family?' she asks him straight out.

'Yes,' Ali admits hesitantly.

Amal hangs up. Ali calls straight back but Amal doesn't answer. She kisses Amina's soft hair and goes on stirring.

She makes a stew for dinner. It's thick and comforting, made with lots of vegetables, chicken and herbs. They eat it with

toasted sourdough bread rubbed with a clove of garlic and drib-
bled with olive oil. Amina starts rubbing her eyes and whining,
so Amal takes her to bed and sings for her until she falls asleep.

Only then does she go back to the living room, take her
laptop and begin searching the internet for her mother.

A week later, she finds a blurry photo on Odnoklassniki,
a Russian version of Friends Reunited. The picture shows a
blonde woman smiling into the camera from a living-room
sofa, a cat in her arms. The woman is older and fatter than
Amal remembers her, but she's definitely her mother.

It takes another two weeks before Amal has the courage to
write to her. She writes in Arabic, although she's no longer sure
Svetlana can even read the language. To be on the safe side, she
gives her phone number in Arabic numerals and not the Indian
ones the Arabs use.

Two hours later, Amal's phone rings. Svetlana starts out in
broken Arabic and then switches to Russian. She trips over her
words, justifying herself, speaking of her many attempts to
contact her children, about the letters she wrote to them, the
Christmas and birthday parcels. When she tells Amal she flew
to Damascus twice and wasn't let into Syria despite her valid
visa, her voice trembles, and as she goes on it gets quieter,
because then she tells Amal she gave up in the end, otherwise
she couldn't have gone on living. Whether going on living was
worth it, she can't say. It's the beginning of a reconciliation.
Something inside Amal starts to heal that day. Over the next
few weeks she tells her mother about Amina and Youssef and
sends photos, but when Svetlana asks how the pregnancy was,
Amal just says there were no complications.

The weather is beautiful, almost too good for the time of year. The sky is clear and idle. Summer has well and truly arrived. Amina is at kindergarten, Youssef will pick her up later. Amal is outside a Syrian supermarket on Sonnenallee, choosing tomatoes, when a man addresses her in Arabic. 'Don't I know you from somewhere?'

She looks up, cautious. Sonnenallee in Neukölln has become a beacon for Syrians over the past few years; they joke that it's now 'Syrian Street'.

'That's a really bad pick-up line,' Amal replies, rolling her eyes and going back to her vegetables.

'But I really do know you,' Hammoudi says with a laugh. Amal looks at him and can't help laughing too now. She doesn't know who he is but his face really does look familiar.

'We met in Damascus. In another life. I picked up a key from you,' Hammoudi says, surprised to find himself remembering this woman.

Amal takes a close look at him and after a while she laughs again and says, 'Oh yes. I thought you were a secret-service man.'

'There's a new pastry shop across the road. Can I treat you to something, perhaps? Only if you have time,' Hammoudi suggests, and Amal nods.

Hammoudi and Amal spend several hours together, during which time Amal is relaxed and calm. The pastry café is simple enough, the floor all white tiles and the walls the same. The sophistication is all down to the pastries themselves, which genuinely taste exactly like they do in Aleppo. The owner keeps bringing new treats over and the two of them eat everything, even though they're long since full. Glasses of tea steam between them.

At some point Amal puts her hand on the table and Hammoudi reaches for it absent-mindedly. When he realizes what he's done he takes his hand back and stutters an apology. He blushes as Amal gets up and asks him whether he'd like to come with her.

Hammoudi nods. They walk along the pavement side by side, not speaking.

'Where are we going?' Hammoudi asks.

Amal looks surprised and then laughs. 'I don't know.'

They take the underground to a hotel and get a room. When the receptionist sees they have no luggage he can't supress a smirk.

Awkward, they enter the room, suddenly embarrassed in front of each other. The place looks dismal, neither particularly large nor cosy. The only thing that might be considered unusual is the strong smell of disinfectant. Amal puts her handbag down in a corner.

Hammoudi sits down on the bed and Amal looks for the minibar.

'Would you like a beer?' she asks.

'Juice, please.'

She laughs, but not convincingly, and then she takes off her shoes and joins Hammoudi with a can of Coke and a small bottle of peach juice. She sits cross-legged. They still don't know why they trust each other. Perhaps it's because they share the same native language and will probably never see each other again. Amal is embarrassed and avoids Hammoudi's eyes. The peach juice is too sweet; he can't drink it.

After a while she starts talking about her daughter. She tells him about the crossing to Italy, about the Mediterranean and their ship going down, and then she takes a breath and asks Hammoudi, 'Can you keep a secret?'

He nods, knowing he mustn't say a word now; it's not his turn to tell his story. The light outside the window grows dusky.

'I didn't give birth to my daughter. She was on the ship with her mother, but her mother drowned. I kept hold of Amina until we were rescued, and then I didn't want her to grow up in a home. I didn't mean to steal her. But now I can't sleep, I'm scared I'll be found out. I know I have no right to my daughter, and at the same time my greatest fear is that someone will take her away from me. An aunt or a grandmother. We looked for them at first, but then we got so used to Amina that we started covering our tracks.' Amal pauses and looks at Hammoudi. Her eyes are clear, enquiring. 'I've never told anyone. Not even my mother,' she says. Her tone changes when she mentions her mother.

'Perhaps it's better that way,' Hammoudi answers.

'And what's the matter with you?'

'I watched nine hundred and seventeen people die.'

Amal puts her hand to her mouth.

Three weeks later, Hammoudi is transferred from his hostel to a home in the back of beyond. They write each other messages for a while, but at some point Amal stops replying. Hammoudi doesn't want to put pressure on her.

It's the weekend, and one of Amal's now-rare days off. Amina's in a bad mood because she's not allowed to play outside. Amal and Youssef are sitting on the floor building something very big out of blocks, which Youssef calls a castle and Amal calls a museum. At some point, Amina loses interest and snuggles up on Amal's lap. Youssef brings them hot chocolate from the kitchen; it could be an idyllic family scene if Youssef didn't start talking about their problems, Amal thinks. Amina wants to be put to bed now so Youssef carries her over to the bedroom. Amal wraps her arms around her knees and stays on the floor.

When he comes back he sits down next to Amal. She's feeling guilty – she'd like to tell him about Hammoudi but she knows he'd get the wrong idea. Plus, she got an offer from her agent a few days ago, to go to LA and record a pilot episode of her show for the US market.

'Have you thought about the offer?'

'I don't know,' says Amal. She looks tired. She puts her legs up on the grey sofa, undoes her bra and sighs, 'I can't take it seriously.'

'We could start over in the USA. People are already recognizing you on the street. Someone's bound to find out our story sooner or later.'

Rain lashes against the windowpanes with new vigour.

'And they wouldn't in America?' Amal asks.

'They don't take Muslims anyway,' says Youssef, and Amal laughs.

'But what if it's a flop, what do we do then?'

'It won't be a flop,' says Youssef and takes her face in his hands. 'And we can always come back.'

'The pay's incredible,' Amal says, and Youssef lets her go.

'It would be easier for me too. I could work again there.'

'You could learn German.'

'I have learned German, I did the integration course, but after that they sent me to the job centre and then made me take an internship at a fried chicken place.'

'I know,' says Amal, and repeats, 'I know,' as though repeating it might make it alright.

'I don't want to complain, but look, I'd like to go back to work too, and that would be so much easier in English than in German. It'd be better for Amina as well. She'd be an American, not a refugee.'

'That's not the issue here,' says Amal, and then she whispers, 'You just want to cover our tracks.'

Youssef looks her in the eye and whispers back, 'I'm scared someone will take her away from us. What would make them better parents? Being blood relatives? What does that mean? We take care of her day and night. We love her. She's got used to us. I'm not going to let her go.'

'I couldn't bear to lose her,' Amal says.

The rain has stopped and the road is covered in puddles, shimmering in the light of the streetlamps. Hammoudi is at the window of the asylum-seekers' home where he's shared a room with three men for the past two weeks.

It's cramped in there, two of his roommates dozing in their bunks. It smells of sleep. Life here is lonely; they're isolated from the town and the locals and can only leave the home in groups. The boneheads lie in wait for them at every turn. They refer to the people in the home as the local brigade of Islamic State.

There are often violent scuffles but the Nazis have never been in a war, so they usually draw the short straw. Last week, though, they got hold of an Afghan boy. He had gone out alone to get an ice cream, and returned to the home with a broken wrist and several broken ribs.

The men in the home got their revenge later. They armed themselves with anything and everything they could find: sticks the children used to play with, a length of pipe, a broken tennis racquet, a broom, kitchen knives. They set out in a collective.

They found the village Nazis in the market square, where they'd tank up on the local cheap beer every night and listen to loud music. As they let loose on them they offloaded all their aggressions, against Assad, against the Islamists, against the Free Syrian Army, against the traffickers, against the boneheads, against German bureaucracy, against their loneliness. After the fight they carried their heads slightly higher. There was even a smile on their faces. The whole town had seen that they could defend themselves. They were still men, even if they had nothing else left.

Hammoudi spots a figure in dark clothing on the other side of the road. Before he can grasp what's happening, a small home-made bomb with modest explosive force comes flying into the room. He doesn't hear the bang. The windows shatter as the people in the home wake with a start.

The local newspaper will report later that there was only one victim. They'll publish an old black-and-white photo of Hammoudi next to the article. Readers will learn nothing about him other than his age and nationality.

Amal says goodbye to Amina and Youssef at Tegel Airport. If all goes well they'll join her in ten days' time. It's hard for her to leave her daughter behind; they've never been apart for longer than a few hours. She can't stop giving Youssef advice about Amina's eating and sleeping habits even though he knows it already, probably even better than she does.

Seven hours later, she boards a Boeing to Los Angeles at Heathrow. As soon as they've reached cruising altitude and the fasten-seatbelt signs go off, she takes off her shoes, stretches out and falls instantly into a deep sleep.

She wakes with a start when the plane is already making its final descent. She dreamed of Hammoudi; a bad feeling rises within her. She sees the Pacific out of the window, an endless blue surface. The water prompts a sense of disgust in Amal; suddenly she can smell the sea and feel the cold in her limbs. She vomits discreetly into the paper bag in the back of the seat in front of her, at which the flight attendant asks in a latently annoyed tone whether everything's alright. Amal doesn't try to look out of the window again, and she resolves to call Hammoudi as soon as she arrives in Los Angeles.

By the time they reach the airport she's trembling all over. The other passengers in the terminal keep an intuitive distance from her and take their children by the hand as soon as they see her disturbed state.

Amal automatically joins the queue for passport control.

The immigration officer studies her and her visa for a long time and then asks her if she's okay.

She nods, and the officer directs her to the nearest sickbay. Amal ignores his advice.

The other passengers' faces are relaxed. A group of young women in short dresses is huddled in the duty-free shop discussing nail varnish. Amal tries to get hold of Youssef but it's the dead of night in Berlin and he doesn't pick up. Then she calls her mother and Svetlana answers straight away. They've only written sporadic emails since Amal's last call, but this time Amal tells the whole story, she tells the truth about Amina and says she can't stand the sight of the sea now. Svetlana lets her talk until Amal's phone runs out of battery. After that, she feels a little relieved.

She collects her luggage, goes to the information counter and buys a return ticket to Berlin. The travel agent doesn't ask any questions, thankfully, merely swiping Amal's card.

At the check-in desk, Amal asks for a seat as far away from the window as possible.

'Are you afraid of flying?' asks the natural blonde with violet-shaded eyelids.

'Something like that,' Amal murmurs.

At last her flight is announced. She jumps up and hurries to the gate. Amal leaves the USA on the same plane she arrived on. It has been refuelled and cleaned ready to head back. A new crew has come on board.

ACKNOWLEDGEMENTS

My thanks go to my German publishing house Aufbau, especially to Lina Muzur and Gunnar Cynybulk, who made this book possible, and to Constanze Neumann, with whom I look forward to working in future.

I'm grateful for the generous and wise support of Karin Graf.

A big thank you goes to Oneworld Publications, especially to Juliet Mabey and Alyson Coombes, who believed in this book, and Will Atkins who worked so well on it.

And my great gratitude goes to the phenomenal translator Katy Derbyshire, who did an incredible job.

I'd also like to thank Inka Ihmels.

Thank you, Neal McQueen.

My gratitude goes to the Kulturakademie Tarabya and the Robert Bosch Stiftung for their support and to all the women who took care of my children and ran my household while I was writing.

My thanks to all the people who shared their time and knowledge with me, in Germany, Turkey, Lebanon and Greece, to the people who shared their stories with me (without wanting to be named), who answered my numerous questions, and whose help and hospitality made my research and my travels possible.

And above all, thank you to my family and to Ayham Majid Agha.

Oneworld, Many Voices

Bringing you exceptional writing
from around the world

Umami by Laia Jufresa (Spanish)
Translated by Sophie Hughes

The Hermit by Thomas Rydahl (Danish)
Translated by K. E. Semmel

The Peculiar Life of a Lonely Postman by Denis Thériault
(French) Translated by Liedewy Hawke

Three Envelopes by Nir Hezroni (Hebrew)
Translated by Steven Cohen

Fever Dream by Samanta Schweblin (Spanish)
Translated by Megan McDowell

The Invisible Life of Euridice Gusmao by Martha Batalha
(Brazilian Portuguese) Translated by Eric M. B. Becker

The Temptation to Be Happy by Lorenzo Marone
(Italian) Translated by Shaun Whiteside

Sweet Bean Paste by Durian Sukegawa (Japanese)
Translated by Alison Watts

They Know Not What They Do by Jussi Valtonen (Finnish)
Translated by Kristian London

The Tiger and the Acrobat by Susanna Tamaro (Italian)
Translated by Nicoleugenia Prezzavento and Vicki Satlow

The Woman at 1,000 Degrees by Hallgrímur Helgason
(Icelandic) Translated by Brian FitzGibbon

Frankenstein in Baghdad by Ahmed Saadawi (Arabic)
Translated by Jonathan Wright

Back Up by Paul Colize (French)
Translated by Louise Rogers Lalaurie

Damnation by Peter Beck (German)
Translated by Jamie Bulloch

Oneiron by Laura Lindstedt (Finnish)
Translated by Owen Witesman

The Baghdad Clock by Shahad Al Rawi (Arabic)
Translated by Luke Leafgren

The Aviator by Eugene Vodolazkin (Russian)
Translated by Lisa C. Hayden

Lala by Jacek Dehnel (Polish)
Translated by Antonia Lloyd-Jones

Bogotá 39: New Voices from Latin America
(Spanish and Portuguese) Short story anthology

Last Instructions by Nir Hezroni (Hebrew)
Translated by Steven Cohen

Solovyov and Larionov by Eugene Vodolazkin (Russian)
Translated by Lisa C. Hayden

In/Half by Jasmin B. Frelih (Slovenian)
Translated by Jason Blake

What Hell Is Not by Alessandro D'Avenia (Italian)
Translated by Jeremy Parzen

Zuleikha by Guzel Yakhina (Russian)
Translated by Lisa C. Hayden

Mouthful of Birds by Samanta Schweblin (Spanish)
Translated by Megan McDowell

City of Jasmine by Olga Grjasnowa (German)
Translated by Katy Derbyshire

Things that Fall from the Sky by Selja Ahava (Finnish)
Translated by Emily Jeremiah and Fleur Jeremiah

Mrs Mohr Goes Missing by Maryla Szymiczkowa (Polish)
Translated by Antonia Lloyd-Jones

In the Shadow of Wolves by Alvydas Šlepikas (Lithuanian)
Translated by Romas Kinka

Humiliation by Paulina Flores (Spanish)
Translated by Megan McDowell

ONEWORLD TRANSLATED FICTION PROGRAMME

Co-funded by the
Creative Europe Programme
of the European Union

IN/HALF by Jasmin B. Frelih
Translated from the Slovenian by Jason Blake
Publication date: November 2018 (UK & US)

WHAT HELL IS NOT by Alessandro D'Avenia
Translated from the Italian by Jeremy Parzen
Publication date: January 2019 (UK & US)

CITY OF JASMINE by Olga Grjasnowa
Translated from the German by Katy Derbyshire
Publication date: March 2019 (UK) / April 2019 (US)

THINGS THAT FALL FROM THE SKY by Selja Ahava
Translated from the Finnish by Emily and Fleur Jeremiah
Publication date: April 2019 (UK) / May 2019 (US)

MRS MOHR GOES MISSING by Maryla Szymiczkowa
Translated from the Polish by Antonia Lloyd-Jones
Publication date: March 2019 (UK)

Oneworld's award-winning translated fiction list is dedicated to publishing the best contemporary writing from around the world, introducing readers to acclaimed international writers and brilliant, diverse stories. With these five titles from across Europe, generously supported by the Creative Europe programme as well as various in-country literary and cultural organizations, we are continuing to break boundaries and to bring new and exciting voices into English for the first time.

For the latest updates, visit oneworld-publications.com/creative-europe

© Rene Fietzeck

Olga Grjasnowa was born in Baku, Azerbaijan. Her debut novel *Der Russe ist einer, der Birken liebt* (*All Russians Love Birch Trees*) was awarded the Klaus-Michael Kühne Prize and the Anna Seghers Prize. *City of Jasmine* is her third novel. Olga Grjasnowa lives with her family in Berlin.

Katy Derbyshire, originally from London, has lived in Berlin for over twenty years. Her translation of Clemens Meyer's *Bricks and Mortar* was longlisted for the Man Booker International Prize 2017. She occasionally teaches translation and also co-hosts a monthly translation lab and the bi-monthly Dead Ladies Show. Katy was recently awarded the Translator Prize of the Foundation for Art and Culture NRW – endowed with €25,000 – for her translation and advocacy work.